MAX'S CAMPER

A FESTIVAL OF Fear

TYLER RHODES

Copyright © 2024 Tyler Rhodes

All rights reserved. This book or any portion thereof may not be reproduced or used in any manner whatsoever without the express written permission of the author except for the use of brief quotations in a book review.

This is a work of fiction. Names, characters, businesses, places, events and incidents are either the products of the author's imagination or used in a fictitious manner. Any resemblance to actual persons, living or dead, or actual events is purely coincidental.

Dedicated to all the festival-goers. Nobody knows the hardships we face just to watch some live bands and chill for a few days. Yes, I'm talking drop toilets!

Chapter 1

"What do you think, Anxious? Looks good, right?"

Anxious wagged happily from the shade of the sun shelter where he'd spent most of the last five days.

I stepped away from the red and yellow striped windbreak I'd bought from one of the stalls and admired my handiwork. I felt like a real vanlifer now, and was pleased with my festival setup.

Not only did I have Vee, my 67 VW Type Two T1 campervan up on the levelling ramps like all the vanlife pros, but I'd organised my outdoor kitchen under the sun shelter with a windbreak behind it to stop the gas flame blowing out on my portable stove. I'd also got my camping chairs, a folding metal box for fires, and my little coffee table too. It was homely, and had everything I needed—apart from a washing machine and a toilet.

Planning ahead, I'd even had a tent delivered to the cabin where you collected your wristband on arrival, and set that up so when our guest arrived there would be no issue about space. Right now, I was feeling smug and about as happy as a man in a field surrounded by other campervans and a sea of tents could be.

"I can't believe we've been here for five days already. Remember what it was like when we first arrived? It was nearly empty. Now it's rammed. Good job we set up by the hedge, so at least we have plenty of room."

Anxious barked his agreement then lay down, panting because of the heat. I smiled at the little Jack Russell Terrier, my best friend in the whole world and constant companion on my vanlife adventure, then joined him because the temperature had soared to record-breaking heights. It was impossible to be out in the sun for more than a few minutes without feeling like you were melting.

It promised to be an incredible three days of music, food, and generally having an awesome time. Lydstock was open for the entire week and your ticket included a full seven days of camping, but the music didn't start until this afternoon. We'd taken full advantage and come early to relax and watch everything build around us, having a fantastic, laid-back week soaking up the atmosphere and doing nothing but going for walks in the incredible surrounding hills and cooking tasty one-pot wonders in my cast-iron Dutch oven.

Nobody died, nobody got injured, nobody even stubbed a toe. It was pure bliss. I felt rejuvenated, and so relaxed I was almost comatose, but was keening to watch bands and sample food from the various stalls setting up in the main arena up the hill and through the trees.

There was only one thing missing, and that was about to change.

"Guess who's coming to visit for the rest of the week," I teased as I sat beside Anxious. His ear twitched but he remained on his side, drained of energy because of the temperature now thirty-two degrees celsius according to my phone.

I didn't blame him, as it felt difficult to breathe, like the sun had incinerated the oxygen, and it was supposed to get even hotter! It was unprecedented, and the already warm summer had leapt to record-breaking heights, leaving everyone at the festival completely unprepared. There was a rule for music festivals, and it never changed. No matter what the forecast promised, you could guarantee rain, mud, and more mud. The only clothes you needed were Wellington boots, plenty of spare jeans, a thick, woolly jumper, and a waterproof coat. Plus an umbrella or three, as you were guaranteed to lose at least two.

But for the first time ever there was sun, glorious sun, not a cloud in the sky, and the weatherman had even promised it would remain in the thirties the entire week. Such a guarantee was as unheard of as a dry week in July when you wanted to be outside to see the bands play.

We watched people dash from the shade of their campervans or sun shelters to the drop toilets, pinching their noses after gulping down a deep breath then trying to do their business before the air ran out, or racing back to their pitch when they realised they'd forgotten the loo roll. Others were checking the site, little more than a large field now full of endless varieties of tents and homes on wheels.

The great thing about Lydstock was how relaxed things were here. Nobody cared about your pitch size. Everyone was allowed to spread out and take as much room as they wanted, as the festival was limited to a few thousand people and two fields for camping.

The music would be over three stages, the main stage at the top of the site close to the beer tent, with the others hidden away amongst the trees. Stalls had been setting up for the last few days, selling the usual boho and hippy gear, more bracelets than seemed reasonable, beads and crystals, pictures, the usual guy with a chainsaw carving animals and mushrooms like a thing possessed, and this morning when we'd gone up there for a walk, the food outlets were preparing for the hungry hordes. More would arrive throughout the morning, ready for the grand opening at lunchtime.

Having been to numerous festivals over the years, both large and small, this was about as good as it got. Lydstock might not have the big names like at Glastonbury, but it was a nice, intimate vibe where you recognised faces from years past, you could find your way around in five minutes flat, nobody got lost, meaning children were allowed to roam freely as it was like one big happy family, and best of all, dogs were allowed.

Anxious wasn't a fan of loud music, but he adored all the people and the attention he got, so as far as he was concerned it was a fair trade. This year, same as always, I'd brought his doggie earmuffs and he would wear them when we watched the bands and always had a good time once the sound was muted. He also looked very cute as they were bright red and set off his white and brown fur very nicely.

I checked my watch—just gone ten in the morning—and gasped as I licked my dry lips. After applying lip balm, I leaned to the side and opened the lid of the new coolbox I'd bought especially for the festival and would leave with Min once it was over. With a pang of guilt because of the time, but figuring I deserved it as I'd held off on day drinking all week, I pulled out a bottle of beer and took a deep swig.

"Ah, this is the life, Anxious. It doesn't get better than sitting in a field and sipping on a cool beer at ten in the morning with a glorious day ahead."

Anxious tilted his head about a millimetre, yawned, then flopped down again and closed his eyes.

I smiled, truly happy, and took another sip.

"What on earth are you doing?" asked a familiar voice as I jumped awake, almost spilling my beer, and standing like a naughty schoolboy caught dozing in class.

"It wasn't me, miss, it was him!" I accused, pointing at a random guy walking past, thinking I really was in school. Coming back to myself, I realised it was Min standing before me like an angel with the sun at her back, highlighting her sandy-blond hair, trim figure in faded denim shorts and a green vest, smiling happily with her hands on her hips.

"Beer at eleven in the morning?" she asked, eyebrows raised.

"It was beer at ten when I started. I must have dozed off." I stifled a yawn and put my beer down on the small green table, then grabbed Min and hugged her tight. "You smell nice." I took in the familiar scent of shampoo and perfume, my stomach flipping and my heart beating fast as I soaked in her warm body.

"You smell like you've been festering in a field for a week and drinking beer," she laughed, folding her arms around me and hugging tighter.

"I don't know why," I chuckled.

We broke apart and I bent while Min stood on tiptoe, her five five versus my six one meaning we'd got the moves down to a fine art over the years. Max and Min, the irony of our names never lost on me.

"Your hair's grown. How does it grow so fast?"

"Dad's the same. He has his cut every fortnight," I said, running my fingers through the tangle of brown locks now down to my shoulders. "Even my beard's getting long."

"It'll be past your knees soon if you don't trim it."

"I trimmed it yesterday!" I protested, tugging at the hair, wondering if I should try and get a brush through it but figuring that could wait until I showered.

Min smiled happily, then stepped back and inspected me as I stood there, feeling rather self-conscious. "Been enjoying yourself?" she asked, face twitching, full of mirth.

"Yes. Why?" I asked cautiously.

"Because you look like a hobo."

"I am a hobo. And loving it!" I flung my arms wide and laughed, overcome with happiness at having the love of my life here for the next three days. "I'm glad you came."

"Me too. Work has been beyond hectic. I've been snowed under with clients. Everyone wants to look trim for the summer, so my dietitian practice is beyond busy."

"But now you get a nice long weekend off. It's going to be awesome. I don't look that bad, do I?" I glanced down at my admittedly rather grubby cut-offs, my dusty Crocs, and black vest, then looked at Min with hope in my eyes.

"No, you look great. A real hippy vibe, but very handsome. Deep tan, and slim, and I'm sure you're more muscular."

"Thanks," I flexed my biceps and struck a suitably manly pose. "I've been working out every morning, and we've done lots of walking. Although, it's been so hot that we have to go either first thing in the morning or late in the evening. And where is Anxious? He hasn't said hello."

Min and I searched, but the little guy was nowhere to be found.

"He can't have gone far," said Min. "I'm amazed he's got the energy with this heat."

"Me too. He's just been lounging in the shade all week and hardly moving. Although," I sniffed, "I can smell barbecue. No prizes for guessing where the hungry guy is."

We turned as a high-pitched howl of happiness thundered across the field. Anxious came tearing from a collection of tents where a group of punks waved happily, smoke drifting lazily from their barbecue. Desperate to say hello to Min, he weaved between tents, hopped over blankets, snatched a sausage on the run from the outstretched hand of a young woman who laughed, then tore across the access lane and leapt into Min's arms, tail wagging manically. Tongue already primed for some serious chin licking, he proceeded to slobber over Min with unnerving vigour.

"Whoa! Calm down, Anxious!" laughed Min as she tried to keep hold of the wriggling dog as he dribbled over anything within reach. "You stink of sausages and smoke," she teased. "Don't either of you wash?"

"We don't have to wash. We're at a festival," I joked.

Unable to contain Anxious a moment longer, Min stumbled into the shade of the sun shelter and fell onto her perfect rear. Anxious leaped onto her belly and spun in a circle, barking loudly for Min to play.

"I think he missed you."

Min sat up and tried to straighten her hair. "I think you might be right," she giggled, her face flushed and as happy as I'd ever seen her. "Anxious, can you sit so I can stroke your head?"

Anxious sat immediately and his eyes bored into Min's as he trembled with hardly contained excitement. He stretched forward to receive a fuss, then groaned with delight as Min stroked his head and scratched his ears.

Already burning up out in the open, I joined them on the blanket, smiling and beyond content now I had my two best friends with me. The day couldn't get any better, and my heart sang for joy that Min still loved being in my company after the mess I'd made of both our lives, before she'd finally had enough and divorced me a year ago.

Slowly, we'd both clawed our lives back, and were now, if anything, better friends than we'd ever been. I vowed to win her back and had been doing my best ever since to be a better man, admitting my mistakes and doing whatever I could to right the wrongs. Quitting my old life and embarking on a totally new one had felt like the right thing to do once things had settled down, and it was the correct decision. Vanlife was incredible, one-pot cooking every night a revelation, and my newfound role as a man who could solve seemingly unsolvable murder mysteries was my true calling. That's what it was. A calling. The reason I had embraced life as a nomad. Plus, I got to go to so many cool places and meet all manner of interesting people.

"What are you looking so wistful about?" asked Min as Anxious finally calmed down and flopped over onto his side, panting and exhausted, content as only a dog could be.

"Just thinking about how perfect life is."

"And that you haven't had anything awful happen for a few weeks?" Min teased with a raised eyebrow.

"Yes, it's been so relaxing. All the mysteries feel like they were a dream."

"You did so well solving the vet murders. That sounded so wild. Racing around on quads and a showdown at a castle. Incredible!"

"It was epic, yes. But it's been nice to take it easy."

"And now I'm here to make it even better."

"You make every day perfect," I said, meaning it. "But let's make a deal."

"Okay," she said warily.

"No talk about our relationship. No discussing things like do you really need a year to find yourself before we get back together?"

"Max, I..."

"Yes, I know. This is what I mean. We've been over that. You know how I feel, and I know how you feel. You can't wait to have me around again, and Anxious and I know it's inevitable."

"Stop being so silly."

"But for the next few days let's just have fun, not discuss any of it, and eat lots, listen to music, and maybe have a few beers too. Deal?"

"You absolutely have a deal. I'm looking forward to this so much. I love Lydstock. We missed it last year, but I always enjoy coming. This one should be wild."

"It will be. It's the twenty-five-year anniversary so they're pulling out all the stops. Incredible bands, loads more food stalls, there's a circus, lots of performers, and even fireworks on the last night. We'll have a blast."

"That's what I plan on doing. After such a hectic few weeks, this is exactly what I need. Why do they call it Lydstock? Have you found out this year? It's always bugged me."

"Still no idea," I admitted. "I bumped into Benny Nails yesterday and he still wouldn't tell me. "

"Benny Nails," sighed Min with an amused shake of her head. "What a name for a man who runs a music festival. He sounds like he should be an East-End gangster, not an old hippy with farmland he now leaves to the wildlife."

"He's a great character and has gone for it this year. He told me there will be a few surprises and this will be the greatest festival he's ever run. I still can't believe it's so cheap and you're allowed to camp all week at no extra charge."

"He just loves seeing people happy. And I am."

"Me too."

There was a moment's silence as Min glanced at the coolbox and tugged her lip like she always did when worried.

I laughed as I said, "It's okay if you want a drink. I put a bottle of Prosecco in there if you're interested?"

"You know me too well," she said, her dimples making my stomach flip. "Hey, why not? I'm on holiday."

I sorted us both out with a drink, then we sat with Anxious snoring between us and clinked glasses.

"Cheers," we both said happily.

"To Lydstock."

"And to no murders," said Min before taking a sip.

"What did you have to say that for?" I groaned.

"What? You aren't superstitious, are you?" she teased.

"I might not be superstitious, but even I know you don't start the first day of your holiday by saying something like that."

"Don't be daft. What could possibly happen here? There are three thousand people ready for a good time. Nothing will go wrong."

"You just wait," I warned. "You've only gone and jinxed it."

"You're so silly." Min's eyes sparkled as she sipped her bubbly booze.

Maybe she was right.

But then again...

Chapter 2

"Max!" called a familiar voice from across the field.

I smiled as I turned to Min and asked, "Are you ready for this?"

"Of course. He's a hoot. And his band is headlining on the first night. That is so cool."

"Very," I agreed.

Anxious sat up, ears primed, tail wagging as he locked his intense gaze on a man hurrying across the open space, the sun beating down on him ferociously. Luckily, his trilby protected his head of short grey hair from the worst of the sun, but his bare arms were already red. My uncle was a total ska and two-tone nut, and had worn the same style of clothing for as long as I could remember. A few years younger than his brother, my dad, at fifty-two, he was a traditionalist in some ways, a real maverick in others. With his hat, a black Fred Perry polo shirt, and white braces holding up drainpipe jeans he always wore short to show off his white socks and shiny black shoes, Uncle Ernie was the epitome of ska cool.

A slight man, whereas Dad and I were a little wider, he was wiry with what you'd call a lived-in face. He'd been on the music scene for years in various bands when in his twenties, but found his true home with The Skankin' Skeletons, a fusion of full-on, jump around, fun, upbeat music with plenty of punk-inspired interludes. The band had been together for almost thirty years and had played at the festival every year it was on, and no way would they miss this big celebration. Especially because they got to headline this evening.

"Uncle Ernie," I beamed as he hurried into the shade of the shelter.

"Max, so awesome to see you. And who's this gorgeous young lady? You aren't playing around are you?" he asked with a cheeky wink at Min, his laughter lines creasing.

"You're so silly," laughed Min, pecking Uncle Ernie on the cheek.

"Sorry, can't help it," he chuckled. "Great to see you, Min. It's been a while." He left that hanging, as we all knew the situation and that for the first year of our separation things were rather unsettled to say the least; family gatherings with Min present were few and far between.

"It has, but you look younger if anything. New hat?"

"This old thing? No way! That would be like chopping my own arm off. Same hat, same old Uncle Ernie. I'll never forgive my parents for the name though. Who calls their son Earnest when they know damn well what his surname is?"

"You think you have it bad?" I said, shaking my head. "What about me?"

"What about you?" he asked with a frown. Then we burst out laughing as this was a thing we always did, much to Min's frustration.

"So, are you ready for tonight?" I asked.

"Not yet, but we will be. Finally, we get to headline. The guys are stoked. The tickets are sold out, and everyone loves a right good jump around on the first night. It's going to be the best Lydstock ever. But listen, we only arrived an hour ago and have a ton of stuff to do. If we don't catch up later, then we have the weekend to hang out, but make sure you're there tonight."

"We wouldn't miss it for the world. Right, Min?"

"No way. We're so proud of you, Uncle Ernie. You deserve this."

"Thanks," he said, grinning from ear to ear. "It's not like we're headlining Glastonbury, but this place means so much to us, and Benny Nails has always been a staunch supporter. Hey, is my brother coming? Maybe this year?"

"Sorry, but no," I said. "You know he and Mum aren't into this kind of music. It's strictly rock and roll from seventy years ago for them."

"I know, but I just thought maybe this year... Ah well, their loss," he said, seemingly over the upset. "At least my favourite nephew is here with his pretty wife. Er, sorry, pretty ex-wife."

"That's okay. No need to apologise," said Min kindly.

Anxious could contain himself no longer, and even though Uncle Ernie had been fussing over him the entire time, he was yet to have a proper hello. Three staccato barks that echoed around the campsite and set hundreds of dogs to barking was all the impetus my ska-obsessed uncle needed to beam down joyously at Anxious, squat beside him, and tickle his tummy. Anxious was in seventh heaven and rolled over, legs kicking in the air, as his belly was rubbed and his chin stroked.

"Sorry about that, Anxious. You know I love you," he guffawed, his good mood something that never changed. Uncle Ernie was an optimist, and even when life had been tough he remained upbeat. He'd battled through many hardships, including losing my aunty over a decade ago, but had stuck to his music, kept it together, and enjoyed life to the full.

"He missed you. We all did," I said.

"It's been a busy year. New album, touring, now the festivals. Good times. But how is Anxious? How's your paw, boy?"

Sensing biscuits if he played this right, Anxious rolled over, stood, and lifted his poorly leg. Not that there was any issue with it now, weeks after the accident.

"My, you are a brave boy," he said with a wink.

Min tittered into her hand; I shook my head as I smiled at the pair.

"Maybe someone deserves a nice treat? Would that make you feel better?"

Anxious barked, so Uncle Ernie produced a biscuit. Anxious took it gently, retreated to the camper, ducked under, then settled to eat.

"Wow, she's a real beauty," gushed Ernie as he straightened his clothes, adjusted his braces, and gawped at Vee. "I love the orange. It's such a classic. I'm jealous. You'll have to give me the tour, but right now I have to get a move on. Lots to do."

"We've got all weekend," I said. "Good luck tonight. It's going to be great."

"Hope you kill it up there," said Min.

"Thanks. It's so great to see you guys. We'll hang out loads after tonight, I promise."

Ernie made a dash for it into the sunshine while we retreated further into the shade.

"He's so sweet," said Min. "So genuine."

"He sure is. Ernie's a fantastic uncle and a top bloke. I think he's miffed that Mum and Dad couldn't make it, but he knows Mum isn't the best at camping and this isn't their scene."

"She likes to stay clean," frowned Min as she flicked a lump of something crusty from her shorts.

"She does. Imagine her using drop toilets, showering in cold water, and not having a table full of her make-up. She only just got through a night in Vee, let alone in a tent. I said they could have stayed in the camper, but they passed."

"But we're going to have the best time ever!"

As the day wore on, we remained in the shade and watched people come and go. It was always fun spying on first-timers setting up their tents. Struggling with the vague directions, or giving up completely and opting for a beer instead. Campervans and motorhomes of all description arrived, with people erecting awnings, settling into their stay, while scores of children ran around, plastered in sunscreen, red-faced and happy to have the freedom.

We chatted about this and that, keeping the tone light and the subjects the same, then decided to go and explore the main arena after a light lunch and a doze. We joined a steady stream of excited festival-goers as we plodded up the track through the trees, the shade welcome, then dashed across open ground once past security and into the woodland stage area. There would be no bands here until this evening, but the main stage up by the beer tent was already rocking with a moderate crowd. Things would get going properly this evening, but the atmosphere was already buzzing, people excited as much by the prospect of three days of freedom from jobs and worry as by the anticipated acts.

We watched the energetic trio for a while from the shelter of the beer tent, then got ourselves a drink and slowly made our way around the various stalls and food outlets, of which there were plenty. I was salivating as we passed food options from around the world, as well as the usual wood-fired pizza and chip van options. I used to struggle with such offerings, the chef side of me taking over, finding fault with the choice of ingredients, the portion size, the provenance, but had mellowed over the years, and thanks to Min accepted that not everything had to be fine-dining or served on a plate more expensive than the meal.

Michelin three-star standard it was not, and that was the whole point! To celebrate street food, about as authentic as it came. Many of the stalls were manned by generations of families, with recipes handed down from mother to daughter or father to son, often with an elderly relative overseeing the operation with a beady eye, perched on a white plastic chair.

"You're doing very well," said Min with a knowing smile and a squeeze of my arm.

"Thanks. No more being judgemental or balking at the prices. I'm just soaking it in and having a fantastic time. Especially with you here."

"Isn't it great? The atmosphere is different this year. It's always upbeat, but this year it's like everyone is mega happy."

"It's because it's the anniversary and the sun's shining. It's unprecedented."

"So let's have the most fun we've ever had."

"I intend to."

We wandered around some more, no rush, saying hello to familiar faces, meeting new people, chatting with the food vendors and promising we'd try out their wares over the ensuing days.

There was magic in the air, and everywhere you looked people were laughing and joking, smiling happily, eating food, drinking, dancing, and generally having the best time ever.

Above all else, it felt safe. The hired security were present but unobtrusive, nobody was causing trouble, and because of the size of the festival children were allowed to roam freely. It was small enough that they could easily find their parents or go wait at the meeting point if they lost their bearings.

The small circus was a firm favourite with the kids and adults alike, with shows and free things to try. Hula hoops were scattered around the big top, along with unicycles, diablos, and the people running it were dressed up in bright clothes and more than willing to help anyone that asked.

We even watched a Punch and Judy show, taken aback by the violence, but we laughed along with everyone else as we sat on the hard benches with Anxious straining to see so he could keep an eye on the sausages that kept making an appearance. We held hands the entire time. I couldn't have been happier.

I forwent a one-pot wonder for this first evening and instead we drank wine at the camper then headed back up to watch the bands and sample the food offerings. I went for Cajun chicken after being promised it was free range, and Min had Caribbean pork with rice and beans. Both were excellent, and filled us up, if rather overpriced, but that wasn't fair as there was never any telling if the vendors would do good business or sales might be flat. A lot depended on the weather. This year they were in luck, and despite the heat people were flocking to the stalls and business was brisk.

Soon it was getting dark, the evening having flown by, so I put Anxious' earmuffs on him and we moved closer to the stage so we had a prime spot for Uncle Ernie and The Skankin' Skeletons. Thousands had the same idea, and soon it was packed. We decided to move further back up the brow of the hill and closer to the sound and lighting engineers' booth where Anxious wouldn't get squashed. We had more room to dance and he could see, too, so it wasn't a problem.

Suddenly, the lights dimmed to deafening applause. When they didn't come back on, people began to question if there was a problem. Min and I exchanged a worried look, the light from the booth enough for us to see each other.

As I turned to check what the engineers were doing, a single deep bass chord rang out as the entire festival lit up with blazing white light before we were plunged into darkness again.

Smoke hissed from machines on the stage as a creeping spotlight passed left to right, then a dull orange light was added, casting everything in an eerie glow.

Min and I smiled. We knew Ernie and the band had put considerable effort into their headline act, practising for months as well as co-ordinating with the engineers to ensure this was a performance to be remembered.

Ominous death march music blared tinnily from the speakers, scratchy music like it was on old vinyl, adding to the suspense as everything went dark once more.

And then...

BOOM!

The stage lit up with lights strobing, spotlights on the seven band members, all of The Skankin' Skeletons wearing matching white Fred Perry polo shirts, black ties, black braces, dark jeans, with trilby hats. Their arms were painted white, with skeleton make-up on their faces, deep shadows from the overhead harsh white light and the roaming greens and reds making them look both freaky and utterly magnificent.

And then we were off. The trombone blared, drums beat deep and loud, and the bass got into your bones. The familiar, unmistakable rhythm of ska took hold as it soared into the night sky, and I couldn't have kept my feet still if I'd wanted to.

Min and I beamed at each other then shouted for joy as Uncle Ernie grabbed the mike from the stand, pointed right at us, and roared, "This one's for Max, Min, and Anxious!" Then he belted out one of their classics and the crowd went truly wild.

People cheered, sang along, and danced their hearts out as the seven-piece ska lovers gave it their all. Lights strobed, smoke billowed, and Ernie jumped about with the others, enjoying themselves as much, if not more, than the rest of us.

As the first song ended, the applause was deafening. The Skankin' Skeletons waved from the stage, already sweating under the lights and the insane night temperature on the hottest day of the year. Their macabre make-up was running, but if anything it added to the undead vibe, a delightful play on the upbeat nature of their music, but an image that had stuck with them for decades ever since they realised they were wiry guys and would remain that way because of their love of dancing.

Although hard to believe, the next song was even better, and the third a manic affair that upped the tempo and left jubilant fans screaming for more as they sweated their way to ecstasy.

Track after track improved on the previous, the band now soaked through, grinning like devils as the lighting technician worked some true magic and gave them the best show of their lives. The sound was perfect, the stars had come out, and people were smiling and clapping as one of the most overlooked ska bands the country had ever produced finally performed a show that did them and the audience justice.

Ernie careened around the stage like a thing possessed, his raspy vocals and energetic style perfect but never overbearing. He gave the others plenty of limelight, bringing them forward and showcasing their skills one by one throughout the set. Even the young guitarist, new to the band as the usual guy had been struck ill, had performed almost flawlessly, if looking rather stage-struck by the attention.

The finale began, with Ernie whipping the crowd into a frenzy, everyone skanking wildly as a ska punk favourite burst from the speakers. The lighting guys surpassed themselves as we approached the crescendo and Ernie flung himself about with wild abandon, while the drummer beat on the drums manically and the rest pushed their instruments to their limits.

The stand-in guitarist turned to his left and let loose with a raging flurry of screeching, angry chords that sent revellers to new heights of skanking. Utterly carried away, he stage-dived and was held aloft by the dense crowd then deposited over the barrier before dashing back on to the stage and letting rip with an energetic solo as Ernie clapped to the manic beat.

Sparks flew from the guitar and amp, literally, as the strings were strummed, then a small speaker burst into flames and everyone cheered and cat-called as the last chords rang out. The guitarist struggled to unfasten the strap, then smashed the guitar over the speaker. He pumped his fist, then spasmed and dropped like a stone as the last beat of the drum sounded.

Ernie flung his arms above his head and roared, "Thank you, and goodnight!" Smoke machines belched dense clouds, the curtains closed, and the lights snapped off, plunging us into darkness as the audience applauded and whistled.

More mellow lighting blinked back on and although there were loud calls for an encore there was none, so slowly people drifted off, talking animatedly as they headed either for bed or, more likely, the beer tent.

As Min gushed about the music, I felt oddly tense. It was a set to die for, and I worried it might have been taken rather too literally. We battled our way towards the front, then around the side where a security guard let us through to backstage where I led Min, my speed increasing, until we were on the stage.

Everyone was talking at once, then a medic barrelled past us. As we arrived, the medic stood, turned to the band, and said, "I'm sorry, but he's dead. Stand clear."

Min and I watched with the others as the soaked guitarist was given several electric shocks, the paddles making his body convulse, but it was obvious it was no use, and soon enough he was pronounced dead.

It had been a killer set. Literally.

Chapter 3

Anxious whined and backed away. Stressed, he bumped into the smouldering remains of the speaker, hopped sideways, caught himself in the tangle of the broken guitar, slumped down, and whimpered. I scooped him up and stroked his head until he calmed, then settled him away from everyone and explained that we wouldn't be long.

Returning to the others, I put my arm around Ernie and asked, "You okay? What happened?"

"I have no idea," he panted, sweat glistening on waxy skin. "We figured he'd rigged something up with the amp," he shrugged. "Lad was very keen, and very skilled."

"Not that much of a lad. He was twenty-nine," said Skully, the drummer. "I saw the amp blow and the cable was showering sparks, then he struggled out of the guitar and smashed that burning speaker."

"It wasn't part of the set?" asked Min.

"No. The gear's too expensive to destroy. He's really dead?" Skully asked the medic.

"I'm afraid so. Ah, here's my colleague. Please give us some space. This is a big shock. Maybe you should rest? That was a very energetic set. Incredible, actually." The medic smiled in sympathy at the band, then moved off to discuss things with his colleague before they both returned to the body and performed more checks.

"This is unreal," said Ernie numbly, rubbing at his face then removing his hat and staring into space as he turned it over in his hands repeatedly. "Poor Dutch. He had a bright future ahead of him."

We stared down at Dutch. He was soaked through like everyone else. The gruesome make-up had run so much there was little left but black and white smears, and his clothes were smouldering. His face was ashen, eyes now closed, but his hands were burned and bent rigid like claws.

We moved back to by the drums and out of the harsh glare as engineers fiddled with lights to assist the paramedics.

"Someone murdered our temp guitarist," hissed Ernie, fists bunched until he realised he was ruining his hat, which he put back on.

"Don't be daft, Ernie," said Chaos Charlie the bass player. The other members, Doc Crocs on keyboard—a man after my own heart as he wore nothing else—Skully on drums, plus Sir Reelington, aka Dave, and Sizzlin' Stu, the trombonist and saxophonist respectfully, all grumbled in agreement.

"Charlie, I'm telling you, someone killed the kid. Look at him. He basically caught fire."

"You don't catch fire from a faulty wire," noted Skully, glancing over his shoulder at Dutch.

"No? Then how come he did?" asked Ernie.

"Guys, cool it. We just played the set of our lives, and I know it's awful about Dutch, but c'mon, how awesome was that? We rocked. Best gig ever," gushed Sir Reelington. "I was on fire." Everyone gawped at him as he beamed at us. When Sir Reelington, aka Dave, failed to realise his blunder, everyone groaned then turned away. "What did I say?" he frowned, then smiled as he realised. "Oops!"

"Dave, stop being an insensitive muppet," warned Ernie. Then he grinned, too, and admitted, "We did nail it tonight, lads. Everyone played flawlessly. The crowd was amazing, and the sound and lighting guys did us and themselves proud."

"We rocked," agreed Skully.

"Yeah, but someone still murdered our guitarist," said Ernie woefully. He turned to me and asked, "You'll find out who did this, won't you, Max? It's your thing. You've got a new line of work now and that's uncovering killers. I heard about it from Jack. Your dad sure does love to boast about his boy."

"It's not work. More a calling. Everywhere I go, I get immersed in one crazy thing after another, but yes, I have solved a few murders lately."

"But this wasn't murder. It was a dodgy wire," insisted Skully. "Oi, you," he shouted, catching the attention of a sound engineer in the wings. "Over here." He beckoned the man over. A tired guy in his thirties with wild, frizzy hair, cargo shorts, and a black vest.

"Sorry about your friend. That was nasty."

"Nasty? Nasty! It's your bloody fault. You're meant to check the equipment and ensure it's safe," raged Skully. "The kid's dead because of your dodgy efforts. You killed him."

"Whoa! You can't accuse me. Me and the team are pros. We go by the book. Otherwise, it would be our jobs. I checked that amp personally. I plugged it in, but the lead was his. I can't be blamed if he used a dodgy lead. And don't blame me for the speaker. If people chuck beer on things, they can short-circuit."

"Then let's go and have a look, shall we?" hissed Skully.

"Fine. Let's," growled the engineer.

We crowded around the smashed equipment and the damaged amp that was now turned off. The engineer inspected the amp and the lead, sucking on his teeth as he muttered to himself. "It's all good. No problem I can see with any of it."

"What about the guitar?" asked Ernie. "There has to be something."

"Ernie, and you, Skully, it was an accident. Probably the humidity and sweat. Plus, people were throwing bottles of water to help us cool down. Water and beer were flying everywhere. And we all had a few drinks. It was an accident. Something short-circuited." Dave held his hands out, pleading with the others to calm down, but Ernie and Skully were having none of it despite everyone else's protestations.

"What about the guitar?" asked Ernie. "Check that please," he asked the engineer.

We had to stand back as the paramedics put Dutch onto a stretcher, covered him over, then took him away, explaining that he'd be taken to the hospital despite him being dead, and that most likely the police would be here in a moment because they were currently the other side of the site dealing with another issue.

After they'd gone, with the mood darker than ever, we watched as the technician gathered up the pieces of guitar then sat on the stage floor and checked things over. He shook his head and said, "Nothing. Just a broken guitar. There's no sign of foul play. It was an accident. Never heard of it happening, but this weather is playing havoc with the equipment. Something must have shorted, or there was a power surge, and he was just unlucky. Most likely, he had a weak heart and the shock killed him. There's no way this was down to me or my crew."

"Ernie, I think it's time to get you and the others out of here," said Min softly. "Come on, let's go and have a drink and you can cool down. You're overheating."

"Yes, maybe you're right," conceded Ernie. "Sorry everyone. I'm so damn sad that Dutch is gone. Kid was so full of life, and a wicked guitarist. Such a shame."

"Maybe it was an accident," said Skully, the others nodding knowingly to him and Ernie.

The guys hugged and slapped each other on the back, but the mood was soured by such a terrible thing. As we stepped away, something silver caught my eye. I bent to retrieve it, then thought better and just crouched.

"What's this?" I asked the engineer as he turned to leave. He spun and came beside me as the others closed in. "Don't touch it, but what is it?"

"Looks like a... nah, it can't be."

"Like a what?" I asked.

"A wire you get on tasers. See, there's the bit that clips onto you and the wire there leads to the taser itself. But it's been cut off, just the wire left."

"So are you telling me that someone tasered Dutch and that killed him?" asked Ernie as he crouched beside me.

"It might have short-circuited the amp if it was a strong enough current, or they threw water on the guitar when they tasered him."

Suddenly everyone was having second thoughts about this being an accident. I'd known straight away it was foul play. It always was. I didn't know what made me think that yet, but knew to trust my instincts. I'd seen or heard something that made me sure this was no accident. Now I had to find out what that was. Years working as a chef at the top of my game meant I had an uncanny eye for detail and minutiae, always striving for perfection, and it had come as a surprise to discover how well my skill set translated to uncovering the truth behind a series of grisly and often at first unfathomable murders.

Two officers arrived, so after finally untangling the story once it was left to Ernie to explain, we showed them the taser lead and clip.

The seasoned officer, a man with a thick white beard and matching steely buzz cut, sighed as he stood, knees creaking, and shook his head as he surveyed us one by one. His dark eyes hinted at amusement although he made sure not to smile.

"I'm sorry to break it to you, as you seem to want an answer that isn't yet forthcoming, and are keen for intrigue, but that isn't a taser cable and clip. That's not how they work or what they look like. It's a crocodile clip and a simple cable from a lanyard. Look." He showed his own lanyard, then the engineer lifted his, the band members retrieved theirs from a pile of clothes and assorted phones in a plastic box, and each grumbled once they realised the officer was right.

"I would like to know everyone has their lanyard intact," said the officer. "I'm no detective, but it's a place to start. According to the paramedics, this was most likely death by electric shock, although we won't know for sure until someone from the coroner's office arrives. It shouldn't be long."

Once the lanyards were found to be intact, the officers took names and details, asked the men on security to keep the scene guarded, then told Ernie that Dutch's next of kin would be informed and that he would receive a call once more was known about the death.

One by one, with a few tears shed and several hugs, the others left, until only Ernie remained with us.

Now it was calmer, Anxious came over and sat beside him on the dirty floor, where Ernie had just plonked himself, unable to muster enough strength to remain standing. Min and I joined him, but as I sat a very large security guard sauntered over and smiled.

"How you folks doing?" he asked, his Birmingham accent making it clear he was a Brummie.

"We've been better," mumbled Ernie. "But not as bad as poor Dutch."

"That the guy's name?" he asked, thumbing a hand to the trashed guitar. "From Holland, was he?" he asked brightly, his round features twitching when he smiled, seemingly his default setting.

"No, he was from Carlisle. But his mum was Dutch and when he was young he had a thick accent, so it stuck. I think he was called Peter, but everyone called him Dutch."

"Ah, I get it! Just like me," he beamed. When nobody asked him what he meant, he redoubled his smile, and said, "They call me Moose, as in, er, the animal."

Unable to help myself, the others seemingly the same, even Anxious, we looked up at this gentle giant of a man. He was easily six four, utterly dwarfing Min and Ernie. He had baby features that made it impossible to tell his age. He could have been twenty-one or late thirties, but judging by the way he spoke and his bright and innocent demeanour, I'd guess mid-to-late twenties.

With smooth skin freshly shaved, short blond hair with dark roots, but natural as far as I could tell, and with huge hands and boots bigger than Skully's drum kit, he certainly didn't look grizzly. Even with the high-vis jacket, black army combat trousers, and matching black shirt all the security wore, he wasn't very intimidating once he spoke. Yet I had no doubt he could handle himself and could stop trouble with a look; you wouldn't want to risk one of those meaty hands grabbing you, or worse.

"Nice to meet you, Moose," I said.

"You're confused by me, aren't you?" he chortled, his entire frame shaking, the clothes unable to hide just how overweight he was. "I look the part, but sound like a Brummie kid. I'm twenty-four and can beat anyone in a fight, but I don't enjoy violence."

"So you became a security guard?" I asked, intrigued.

"Course! Stands to reason, doesn't it? The size of me, it's the perfect job. I get to travel all over for events, the gang are a great bunch of guys and gals, and I even get sweet gigs like this one with awesome music and even better people. There's hardly ever any bother, and if there is I deal with it." Moose cracked his knuckles menacingly, but his broad smile and open manner didn't give quite the effect he'd anticipated.

Anxious barked a greeting and Moose was almost beside himself as he scooted over and squatted with a huff to pet him, nearly flattening Anxious as a heavy hand stroked his back like a road roller over tarmac.

Deciding he'd better join us, although it seemed rather odd, Moose sat, the stage vibrating as his twenty plus stone settled. "So, who do you reckon killed him?"

"What?" I spluttered. "Why do you think it was murder? The paramedics said it was probably electrocution, so why would you think differently?"

"I, er, couldn't help overhearing you talking, and looked you up, Max. You're a popular internet meme."

"I'm not a meme! I'm a real person."

"That's not what a meme means," said Min patiently.

"I meant, I'm not just whatever people say about me online. What do they say?" I asked, having ensured to avoid reading any of the stories I'd been involved in for fear of getting sucked into arguing with trolls on forums or possibly starting to believe that the internet was even real. It wasn't. It was just robots, and maybe a handful of living people, but they were all in private groups or on Twitter, although apparently it wasn't even called that anymore.

"They say that you're an ex-chef turned vanlifer who drives about the country in a 67 VW solving murders. Even the police hate you as you make them look bad, but the local communities have built shrines and now have the day off work to celebrate when you solved the crime for them."

"Really? That's pretty cool, actually," I said, unable to hide my pleasure.

"I'm just messing with you!" chuckled Moose, slapping me playfully on the back.

It was like being hit by, well, a powerful bloke with a shovel for a hand, and I slammed sideways into the floor, smashing my face into the dirty boards as something cracked in my back.

"Sorry, sorry, I forget how strong I am. I was only being friendly. Let me help you up." Moose bunched his hand around my vest and righted me with little to no effort on his part. Whatever had cracked before cracked again, but it felt like it went back into place and I could move freely, so it was all good.

"That's some power you have there, kiddo," marvelled Ernie. "But let's be serious. What makes you think it was a murder?"

"Because I know the engineers really well and they're beyond professional. We end up at a lot of the same jobs. And I also know you can easily die from an amp. Especially the old ones. Are your amps old?"

"Older than us," said Ernie, scooting closer, suddenly interested in what Moose had to say.

"They stay live and charged for months, even unplugged. Could be the amp did it," shrugged Moose. "If Dutch was barefoot and the floor was very wet, he could get a massive shock. Was he barefoot?"

"No," said Ernie, deflated.

We eyed the amp suspiciously, but it looked like a regular piece of equipment and the engineers hadn't said there was an issue.

Sighing, Ernie rubbed his face, looking exhausted, then his phone rang. He answered, leapt to his feet, and moved to the back of the stage where equipment was being carted away by the crew. We remained silent until he returned, and he loomed over us, face drawn, as he said, "That was the police. Apparently, they've had a preliminary look at his body already as the coroner's assistant was in the area, and it wasn't death by electrocution. That was most likely just a few sparks from the water flying around."

"So it wasn't murder?" asked Min with relief, glancing at me.

"Oh, it was murder for sure. Someone stabbed him."

Nobody said a word for a moment, letting it sink in, so I had to ask the obvious question. "How could Dutch be stabbed when he was on stage in front of thousands of people the whole time?"

"That, my genius nephew, is a very good question and one I hope you find the answer to very soon. There's no doubt about it. Dutch was stabbed, now he's dead, and someone at this festival is the killer."

"Wait, this doesn't make sense," I insisted. "Where's the blood? Why wasn't he shouting and screaming? Where was he stabbed?"

"Here, on stage," snapped Ernie. "Sorry, but I already said."

"I meant, where on his body?"

"They didn't say, but the police are coming back right now. We need to wait here."

They arrived a moment later.

Chapter 4

Two officers, a security contingent, plus a petite but instantly intimidating middle-aged detective with glorious red hair and a sour face arrived and the scene became strictly business. We were ushered to the rear but told to wait while they sealed off the area and did a thorough search. The festival photographer took pictures as directed by the detective then was asked to move aside.

We watched and waited while they went about their business. Moose came and went, talking to those on his team, then updating us when he could. Finally, only the detective remained, and she marched over to us, her black high heels clicking on the beer-soaked stage.

"I'll get straight to the point," she said curtly, giving Min and Ernie a cursory glance then focusing her considerable distaste on me. It was dislike at first sight, entirely mutual, as this wasn't the attitude I had come to expect, even if I was then warned off from the case.

"What's with the tone?" asked Ernie.

"Him," she grunted, jabbing a finger my way. "Let me make one thing very clear. I hate mud, I hate camping, I hate festivals, and I hate people interfering in my case. Especially the general populace. Do not get in my way, and do not stir up trouble," she warned, slitted eyes locked on me.

"A man was murdered. Can we focus on that?" I asked, keeping my tone level. "But this was a close friend of my uncle's, and I'm within my rights to ask questions like anyone else."

"As long as they don't interfere with police business," she snapped.

"And who exactly are you?" Min glared at the detective, hands on her hips.

Incredibly, the detective didn't spontaneously combust, but even Ernie and I took a step to the side for fear of her intensity catching us alight. Anxious did the smartest thing and stood behind me, out of the range of her laser vision.

"Detective Sergeant Kate Moss."

"Like the model?" asked Moose as he appeared from nowhere.

"Yes, like the model," sighed Kate Moss. "Why are you here?"

Moose, seemingly immune to DS Moss' attitude, smiled warmly and said, "I'm helping."

"Oh, well, that's great. I may as well go home and return to my nice evening. It's my first day off in a month tomorrow, and now it seems like I can relax and open a bottle of wine."

"Sounds nice," said Moose with a nod.

DS Moss shook her head, then scowled at Moose before snapping her head around and locking eyes on me again. "I know all about you, and I won't have it. This is an official investigation, and by the looks of it not a very difficult one to solve. I want to make this clear. No tampering with evidence or causing trouble."

"Don't you mean murder investigation?" I asked.

"No, I do not. There was a puncture wound to the deceased's inner thigh that one of the officers wrongly reported as a stab wound." She shot a glare at the waiting officer who shrank in on himself and suddenly found his shoelace untied, then huffed as she turned back to us. "I've gone over the scene, and this stage is a death trap. It needs to be sorted before tomorrow or there will be no more festival for anyone."

"What are you talking about?" asked Ernie. "Benny Nails runs a proper festival. He's done it for years."

"Follow me," DS Moss sighed. "But I'm warning everyone. This is the first and last time I share my investigation."

We joined her at the front of the stage and she called out into the dark for a light. A spotlight lit up the stage, almost blinding us, then she bent and beckoned us closer. "There. You can see the blood, and to the left here is a jagged piece of metal from the rigging for the lights. See that bolt? It's sheared off, and from what I have been told, this Dutch fellow had his leg up on the front here playing his guitar. It's soaked in beer and water and the blood ran down his leg, over the speakers, and trickled through the boards. It's a simple case of death by misadventure."

"You what!?" shouted Ernie.

DS Moss ignored him. "I'm sorry for your loss, but that's it, case closed. Benny Nails is lucky he doesn't get shut down, but it better be fixed by tomorrow. Sorry to disappoint you macabre amateur detectives, but the poor man cut his leg open and bled to death because he was so hyped on adrenaline he didn't even notice he was injured. By the time the amp gave him a mild shock because of the water and beer being thrown about, it was already too late. Case closed."

"That's... ridiculous," stammered Ernie. "He would have realised."

"Then what's your explanation? That rather than a sheared bolt piercing his femoral artery, he was stabbed there? Why would he not notice that either? No, there's blood all over, although it's mostly washed away, but it's an open and shut case. We are done here."

With a curt nod, DS Moss stormed off, the officers trailing in her considerable wake.

The lights clicked off, leaving us plunged into darkness for a moment before the low level lighting allowed us to see once our eyes adjusted.

"We don't believe that, do we?" asked Moose.

"Where did you come from this time?" asked Min, frowning.

"I'm light on my feet," he said happily. "Max, tell me this is another one of your cases? Can I be in the gang? Help you solve it?"

"Moose, I'd love your help, but it doesn't look like there's a case to be solved," I said.

"Nonsense," said Ernie. "That detective doesn't know her bum from her elbow, excuse my French."

I smiled at Uncle Ernie's choice of words. He was very conservative when it came to bad language and never cursed. It had rubbed off on the others, too, and for a bunch of wild ska punks they were very well-mannered.

"Fine," I admitted. "I don't believe she's right. She hates it here and wants to get home. It's obvious it wasn't the bolt. Look." I moved forward and got close to the bolt on the rigging, then lifted a leg onto the speakers lining the front of the stage. "Dutch was only an inch shorter than me, but look where the bolt is. It's up at my waist. Unless he jumped up and landed on the thing, no way was it the metal. Plus, if it looked like a stab wound, that means it went in deep and the wound wasn't ragged. It would be if he tore his flesh scraping down on it. She's wrong, and couldn't be bothered."

"That's very unprofessional," said Ernie with a frown.

"Maybe not," said Min. "Everyone was very energetic, so he could have jumped and banged into the metal."

"Possibly, but I think we know better, don't we? Someone murdered Dutch and it's down to us to solve this," I said.

"Yes!" cheered Moose as he fist-pumped the air. "Sorry, I didn't mean it like that. I'll leave you guys to it, but sorry for your loss. I'll hook up with you tomorrow and in the meantime I'll ask around."

We said our goodbyes to Moose, then went over things again just to be sure. The DS could have been right. The metal was certainly sharp enough, but the height was definitely wrong.

"We need to solve this for Dutch's sake," insisted Ernie. "He was a good lad and now he's gone. Max, you will help, won't you?"

"Of course I will. I can't understand why the DS was so dismissive."

"It's because this makes no sense otherwise. She's working on the assumption that the most logical answer is the correct one, but we know that isn't always the case," said Min.

"We sure do," I agreed. "So, where does this leave us? With a murderer in our midst, no idea how they did it, and no possible motive. He was a stand-in, wasn't he?"

"Just for the previous gig and today and tomorrow," said Ernie, looking like he could fall asleep at any moment. "He was a great player, though, and we were thinking about adding him to the line-up permanently. As to who might have a motive, I know exactly who that might be."

"Who?"

"The Third Skatallion. They've been after a headline gig here for years, same as us, and were annoyed as hell when they found out we got it. There's been rivalry for years and years, right back to when we first formed. I tried out with them, and played with the original line-up for a while, but we didn't get on. I left, and Doc Crocs came with me, then we formed our own band. Although, back then Doc Crocs was just Doc as Crocs hadn't even come out. They've hated us ever since. Tried to mess up our gigs, even sabotaged our van a few times when we played the same places."

"You think they're capable of murder? Who in the band would do that?"

"Only one person in that third-rate band is mean enough to kill, and that's Major Two-Tone," said Ernie ominously.

"Were they here tonight? Was he?"

"Oh yeah, right at the front, watching us. They steal our ideas, copy our music, and are always studying what we do so they can try to be as awesome as us. The Third Skatallion are bad news, but the others are mostly alright. But Major Two-Tone is an absolute beast of a front man. He'd murder his granny if it meant he could headline. This is his way of getting us scared, or maybe give up entirely. But he's out of luck, because the show must go on and we have a nice chilled afternoon gig on the small stage tomorrow for some gentler vibes. We'll be there. You can count on it."

"Are you sure that's a good idea?" asked Min. "Maybe give it a miss?"

"No way! That's what he wants. We owe it to Dutch to show we don't let vindictive pretend majors frighten us."

"Uncle Ernie, a man's dead, possibly murdered. Don't you think that's reason enough to be careful?" I asked.

"Oh, I'll be careful all right. And I'll wring his scrawny neck." Ernie began to march off, but we caught up and convinced him that now was not the time to go chasing down rival band members. He was having none of it, though, and stormed off the stage then towards the beer tent, determined.

With no other option, we gave chase.

The festival was awash with revellers, many still dancing to their own tune as they sloshed beers, the strong overhead lights casting long shadows across the field. We weaved our way through the thinning throng, trying to keep Ernie in our sights, but lost him almost immediately.

The beer tent was rammed with those who refused to let the night end, and I knew from experience that it would remain packed until the early hours. Old sofas and chairs were bursting at the seams as people rested after the day's festivities, with everyone else packed tightly in the super-heated space.

It was ridiculously hot and I was soaked in sweat immediately. My hair hung into my eyes, my beard was dripping with beer that people kept spilling, and the haze of smoke meant visibility was low.

"I can't see him anywhere," said Min as she tugged limp hair from her red face.

"Me either, and it's impossible to move. Let's wait outside. I can hardly breathe anyway." I got a mouthful of something pungent and it wasn't tobacco, then led Min and a very concerned Anxious away from the press of bodies until we were out in the cooler fresh air and beside the huge marquee.

Raised voices led us around the side of the temporary structure where we found Ernie gesticulating angrily and getting right up in Major Two-Tone's face. The rival front man shoved Ernie and he stumbled towards us, so I dashed forward and caught him before he fell.

Always on guard when it mattered, Anxious bolted between my legs and planted himself between the two men then growled menacingly at the incensed Major Two-Tone, aka Pete, who had begun to come after Ernie.

"Everybody cool it," I said calmly, knowing shouting and getting angry would lead to more problems than it would solve.

"He accused me of murder! Me! The Major doesn't need to kill anyone to get good gigs. The Major already knows he's better than this joker." He jabbed a finger towards Ernie who wriggled in my arms.

"How dare you! You're a joke. Who talks about themselves in the third person like that? And you aren't a major, apart from a major disappointment to your family and the guys."

"No need for that, Ernie," called one of the band. The small group grumbled their agreement, but it was Pete who was the genuinely angry one, the others seemingly oblivious to whatever had already been said.

"He murdered our guitarist. The young lad standing in. He's dead!"

"You what, mate? Dead?" asked another band member, the bass player I think, although I didn't know these men and had only seen them on stage a few times.

"Yes, dead. Right at the end of our last song. You saw the sparks and him collapse. Someone stabbed him and now he's dead."

"We thought that was part of the act. You guys looked great tonight," said a very overweight trumpet player, the fact he was holding his instrument giving the game away. The others turned and glared at him. "What? I was just saying. This rivalry has been going on long enough, and if the lad was murdered then I for one am very sorry."

The others mumbled that they were sorry, too, but still gave the trumpet player nasty looks.

"What about you, Pete?" I asked. "Are you sorry?" I studied him as he adjusted his tie and his stiff army shirt, a look they all shared. With a name like The Third Skatallion, it had to be army themed, and they stuck to it no matter what.

Pete removed his green beret and scratched at his bald head, then frowned as he opened and closed his mouth, no words forthcoming. "I..." he stammered eventually. "Yes, of course I'm sorry he died. Ernie, it wasn't me. It wasn't any of us. We were up here after your first few songs, and can vouch for each other. So don't you come over accusing me of anything. We go way back, sure, and aren't on the best of terms, but murder?" he laughed, shaking his head.

Ernie looked from Pete to the others and asked, "You were up here?"

"Sure," said the trombone player. "We watched from the front for a while, but wanted a beer. Damn good set,

Ernie. You did yourselves proud." Again, he got nasty looks from the band. "Loved the energy and the sounds. Really solid. But we were together. Maybe we nipped inside to get a beer, or went down to the toilets, but that's it. And at the end we were sipping our drinks and then the curtain closed. The lad's really dead?"

"He is," I confirmed.

"And it was murder?"

"We think so, yes," said Min.

All eyes turned to her as she stepped forward beside me, and everything changed in a heartbeat. The guys messed with their hats, straightened their ties, and smiled as they shuffled forward.

"And who's this lovely lady?" asked Pete as he preened like a bird trying to win a mate.

"I'm Min."

"Lovely to meet you, Min," warbled Pete. "They call me Major Two-Tone."

"I'll stick with Pete, thanks," she said, a warm smile plastered on her face, the underlying tone very clear.

Pete was oblivious and held out a hand to shake, so Min shook quickly then moved closer to me.

"And who are you again?" asked Pete.

"I'm with Max," she said, leaving it at that.

"Ah, the ex-wife," crowed Pete, eyes gleaming. It was almost as if this fifty-something thought he had a chance with Min, as he puffed out his bird-like chest and grinned. "Shame you two split up, but let me ask you something, Min. What do you think about singers in cool ska bands? You like ska, right?"

"I love ska, and I like singers in ska bands. Especially this one, because he's family." Min stood on tiptoe, her petite frame glorious. Everyone gasped as she demurely kissed Uncle Ernie on the cheek, her vest clinging to her sweaty body.

"Lucky bugger," mumbled the trombone player.

"Yeah, well, you aren't my type anyway," mumbled Pete as he stepped back and joined his bandmates.

"Did any of you see anything strange at the end of the set?" I asked.

"Like what?" asked Pete.

"Anything? Did anyone get on stage, or did the guitarist do anything unusual? We saw most of it, but with so much going on, and with all the lights, it would have been easy to miss something."

Nobody could think of anything apart from when Dutch had crowd-surfed before clambering back on the stage. The only other time someone could have stabbed him was when the lights went out before the last song, and everyone agreed that had been a good idea and very dramatic for building tension.

Ernie and Pete eyed each other warily, but there was nothing more to be said, so I called for Anxious who gave a leaving warning yip, then we led Ernie away back down into the camping field where the band were set up with a series of tents forming a semi-circle around the tour bus. A large fire was burning in the centre where they were sitting around talking quietly, sipping on beers or smoking e-cigs.

After a few words with them to ensure they'd look out for Ernie and stop him if he tried to wander off, we left, promising to catch up with them in the morning.

Chapter 5

I did not sleep well. Partly due to worrying about Ernie "Elbows" Effort, a man I loved dearly, and partly due to the noise. Festivals are never a quiet affair, and I couldn't find the earplugs, so tossed and turned for much of the night in the tent, very grateful for the self-inflating mattress I'd been dubious about but was surprisingly comfortable.

When I crawled out of the tent at seven to find Min already at the outdoor kitchen, I asked, "Did you sleep as badly as me?"

Min turned, her smile warm and sympathetic, but that was clearly where the similarity between us ended this morning. "I had a lovely sleep. The Rock n Roll bed is really nice. Even with Anxious farting like a, um, fart machine," she giggled, "I slept really well. How was the self-inflating mattress? Did it actually work? It looked like it would be rubbish."

A thin piece of blue material that rolled up into a bag, you merely unscrewed the caps and left it to inflate to a few centimetres. Then you did the caps up and had your very own lightweight mattress. We'd both been suspicious of the rave reviews, but everyone I'd spoken to couldn't say enough good things about them. "It worked incredibly well and I was comfy, but with people partying through the night and the requisite dude on guitar who for reasons that always escape me somehow assumes three thousand people also wanted to listen to his drunken warbling and dubious strumming, a restorative repose it was not."

"Oh, you poor thing. I hardly heard a thing. But then, Anxious was snoring really loudly," Min laughed.

Anxious did a double-take from beside her, then whined before taking one look at me and turning then jumping into the camper. I heard the bed squeak. No prizes for guessing how he planned to spend the morning.

"Why are you so happy at this ungodly hour?" I asked as I stood and my back clicked in a very worrying fashion. I looked at Vee and Min with longing, wishing we could have cuddled up together and been all snug, but prepared to wait if that was what it took.

"Because I got to the toilets first. I had a warm shower, and I found the bacon and sausages in that absolutely tiny fridge."

"You do look nice and clean. You washed your hair?"

"Of course! After last night and getting sweaty and covered in beer, I felt disgusting."

"I was planning on waiting until the next campsite," I mumbled as I tried, and failed, to get my fingers through my tangled beard.

"Max, you can't! You need to shower."

"But who showers at festivals? It's unheard of. You don't even have to brush your teeth when you're away from home."

"Aha, but you aren't, are you? You don't have a shower at home because Vee is your home. So go get cleaned up and make sure to brush your teeth. But my advice is to use the toilets first."

We both glanced nervously over at the row of stalls containing the drop toilets. Basically, it was a converted storage container with homemade doors that didn't close properly and toilet seats on benches with a large pit underneath. Day one would be just about bearable, but by day three you'd be crossing your legs and squeezing your bum cheeks and racing home to proper plumbing and the smell of Air-Wick.

"Good idea. Where's the loo roll?" I asked, pushing down a rising tide of panic as I tried to recall if I'd brought enough.

"Don't worry, I stocked up. Here." Min handed me the loo roll, my wash bag, a clean towel and shampoo, conditioner, then frowned, held up a finger for me to wait, then ducked into Vee and returned with beard oil and my comb. "I like it when your beard's shiny," she said coyly.

"You do?" I asked, grinning.

"Yes, so go get clean. You stink. If you wait, everyone else will be up and you'll regret it. The one thing about rising early at festivals and campsites is the sense of smugness that lasts for hours as you sit sipping coffee and watching everyone else make the 'Walk of Shame' across a field, clutching a damp toilet roll, because you know they know everyone else knows what they're about to do and how gross it is."

"So true," I chuckled, then checked the coast was clear and made a dash for it.

Twenty minutes later, I returned with my badge displayed proudly. "I used a drop toilet and survived," is what it would have said if I really had one.

"You look very handsome," said Min as she inspected me. "Shame about the Crocs, but I'm learning to live with them."

"Best thing for camping, and you can even wear them in the shower," I said smugly.

"At least you don't smell. Did you use deodorant and brush your teeth?"

"Yes, I did. What is this? What are you up to?"

"Nothing. Just looking out for my boys. Anxious has had breakfast, now he's having a nap, so sit yourself down and I'll get you a coffee."

Min whistled as she boiled the kettle and the familiar sounds of making a cuppa left me feeling strangely relaxed after last night's upset. It was because she was here and taking charge. I was a capable man, but it's a wonderful feeling to know that someone else is taking care of you because they genuinely want to. That it makes them feel good as well as you. Doing things for the ones you love just because you can is a true joy and what makes life glorious at times. It might have only been the tinkle of a spoon stirring a mug of instant coffee, but it sounded better than any music I had ever heard.

I settled gratefully into a camping chair, now so used to the flexible, waterproof fabric and the awkward positioning of poles that I didn't even notice it anymore. I couldn't imagine what sitting in a real chair would be like for more than a few minutes. Min placed a steaming mug of coffee in my hands then sat beside me, looking more radiant than ever.

"Thank you. What is it about you this morning? You seem different. Glowing. Aren't you freaked out after last night?"

"No, I'm not freaked out. I guess I'm getting used to this happening around you now. And, as usual, I'm trying to hold back my excitement about the intrigue we're about to get into."

"We?" I asked with a raised eyebrow.

"Of course. For the first time, I get to be here for all of it. I might even solve the case before you," she gushed, voice rising in pitch. "Yes, I might do just that."

"Maybe you will. But that's not it. There's something else going on."

"Max, there isn't. I'm just pleased to have time off work and to spend it with you guys. It feels properly normal for a change. Doing stuff we used to do years ago before work took over and... Anyway, we promised not to talk about us or the past, so enjoy your coffee. Hey, look at that guy!" Min covered her mouth to stifle a laugh as we watched a furtive man crouched over, wearing nothing but a dodgy-looking pair of white Y-fronts and a vest, weaving between tents, using campervans as cover, then making a dash for it across open ground with his loo roll clutched tightly in his hand. He made it to the toilet block, pinched his nose, then raced up the steps and slammed a door behind him.

Soon, more people followed, some trying to brazen it out and holding their heads high, acting like they didn't care that everyone knew their business, but most kept their heads down and their prized toilet roll held tight.

"So, if you're going to solve this, what's your gut telling you so far?" I asked, genuinely interested. "I haven't had the chance to think about this properly yet, but I have a few ideas I want to pursue today. What's your take on it?"

"I'm thinking we can rule out the other band members."

"Why?"

"Um, because why would they do it?" asked Min with a frown, already tugging at her lip.

"Why would anyone? Maybe one of them hated Dutch, or is secretly related, or wants someone else to play guitar. Dunno."

"Max, you aren't playing fair! Fine, let's go over the band members first. We can definitely rule out Uncle Ernie 'Elbows' Effort. Why do they have such silly names?" Min tittered.

"It's to make them memorable and give them an edge. Goes with the ska and punk thing. Can you remember them?"

"Most, but not all."

"We have 'Elbows', Chaos Charlie the bass player, Sizzlin' Stu on sax, Doc Crocs on keyboard, although I don't remember his name as everyone calls him Doc, Skully on drums, Sir Reelington, aka Dave, the trombonist, with Dutch on guitar."

"That's a lot to remember," sighed Min.

"I know, but it doesn't matter."

"Why not?"

"Because I don't think any of them did it either."

"Max! That was mean."

"Sorry. I was only teasing. But we do need to keep Major Two-Tone, aka Pete, in mind, and his band. They have a pretty good alibi, but it would have been easy enough to have left for a few minutes and done the deed. The problem is, we also have three thousand other people who could have done it."

"So where do we start?"

"I want to talk to the DS again. Maybe she was out of sorts last night because of the time and all the people. She might be different this morning."

"Think she'll bother to turn up?"

"My guess is she never left, and is up at the security cabin ensuring that dodgy bolt is fixed and going over the crime scene so there's no blowback about this. She was way too quick to call it, and I bet she's having second thoughts."

"She didn't seem like the type to have second thoughts. She was rude, bossy, and tried to intimidate everyone."

"True, but I still want to talk to her. If nothing else, just to be sure we aren't going to get into trouble."

"Why would we?"

"Because, my beautiful ex-wife, we are going to solve this crime."

"Yes!" Min panicked as she sloshed coffee over her bare thighs, so I jumped up and wiped her tanned legs with a tea towel. I didn't mind one bit.

"Thank you," she said, gasping as I stroked her thigh.

Our eyes met and her colour rose, but I moved my hand and with my back turned, I said, "You're welcome," although it was difficult to speak because I had such a big, smug grin on my face.

"I can hear the smugness," she teased.

"That's okay. I don't care," I said, turning. Our eyes met and we smiled.

Best morning ever!

But then Min ruined it by offering to make breakfast.

"No, let me," I said hurriedly, trying not to sound too keen, or too dismissive of her offer.

"Max, not this again," she said, pouting.

"What? It's just that you've done enough this morning, and you're on holiday. You take it easy."

"You still don't trust me to make a simple fry-up, do you? After all these years, and you think I'm not capable. I burned it once, so long ago I can't even remember—"

"I can," I said with a shudder.

"—but you won't let it lie. I've made plenty since then, and I do it occasionally for myself. I'm cooking!"

Resigned, I spread my arms and said, "Then I thank you," and tried not to grimace.

With a grunt of satisfaction, Min rose and busied herself in the kitchen area just a step away from where I was sitting.

Anxious perked up as Min poked around in the fridge for tiny people, eyes glued on the packs of sausages and bacon as she unwrapped them outside.

"Don't get you hopes up, buddy," I confided with a whisper. "You won't recognise any of it once she's finished massacring our meat. A meat massacrer, that's what she is."

Anxious cocked his head and looked from me to Min, then whined and lay down, having been through this several times before.

I enjoyed it when Min and I cooked breakfast together, but only when she was in charge of beans and the toast, not the frying. She was a fine cook, but for some reason had a problem with sausages and bacon.

We sat. We waited. We crossed our fingers and toes. A foolhardy endeavour, but man and dog were at least doing what they could to mitigate the impending disaster.

Twenty minutes, thirty cuss words, five dropped eggs, three tea towels, and seven plates later, Min gasped, finished dishing up, then handed me my breakfast before she sank into her chair, red-faced and sweating, and focused her attention on me.

"Well?" she asked, eye twitching as she ground her teeth.

Anxious whined from underneath my chair, coward that he was, but I braved it and looked Min in the eye and said, "It looks lovely."

"Liar! You big, fat liar! I can't tell which ones were the sausages, and the bacon fell to bits and somehow got mixed up in the eggs, and they split so there are no runny yokes to dip our toast in."

"Toast looks perfect," I said, noting the pile on the table.

"The toast always looks nice."

"There you go then. Um, where are the beans?"

"On your plate. They got a bit burned, and the sauce vanished somehow, but they're beside the sausage."

"And which one is the sausage again?" I asked, poking at the mushy mess then tasting it. "Yum. Tuck in. You made it, after all."

"Fine, I will!" Min scooped up a mouthful of breakfast and chewed, her face contorting, until she swallowed and said, "There, I ate it."

"Er, well done?" I ventured.

"Now you," ordered Min.

Dutifully, I took a large forkful and let the alien ingredients enter my eating hole with much hidden trepidation. It wasn't actually too bad, and you could certainly taste the bacon, so I swallowed and grabbed a piece of toast then tore off a chunk, sighed with pleasure, and said, "Great job."

"You just meant the toast, didn't you?" she asked, suspicious of me for some reason.

"As if!"

We held each other's gaze in a dangerous game of risk, then both burst out laughing as Min declared, "It's not fair. You were putting me off."

"I was just sitting here," I protested.

"Exactly! Next time, you cook."

"I did offer. But honestly, it's fine. You make some lovely meals, but fry-ups just aren't your thing. You're good at lots of recipes, but we can't all be experts at everything."

"Max, that's just the thing. You are. You excel at everything you turn your hand to."

"I can't believe you're saying that after what I did to the most important thing."

"What's that?"

"You. Us. Who cares about a fry-up? What I did is beyond worse."

"No talking about it," Min reminded me. "But apart from that, you are great at everything."

"Not so. I can't fix Vee if she breaks down. I'm no good with trains as riding them makes me feel weird, and, er, loads of other stuff."

"See, you can't think of anything. It's not fair. You're good looking, smart, and fun to hang out with. You even have a nice beard, and nobody ever has a nice beard."

"Don't they?" I asked, surprised.

"No. But you do."

"Then I admit it. I am awesome. But Min, all joking aside, you are a truly wonderful person and incredibly smart. You're caring, considerate, forgiving, but tough too. And damn pretty."

"Oh, Max!" Min dropped her cutlery and covered her face with her hands.

"What did I say?"

"Nothing. It's just so kind of you to say so."

"Kind of me to say nothing? Eat your breakfast," I ordered, winking.

Min dried her eyes and we forced our way through the gunge of meat and beans, laughing every so often as we enjoyed our time together.

Chapter 6

Washing up was a nightmare. I used way more water than I'd have liked because of the grease, having to refill the bowl multiple times and decanting it into the sink each time. There were certainly drawbacks to this life, but they were worth the sacrifice. Rather than move the campervan from its levelling ramps, something that took an age to accomplish, I dragged out the grey water container from under the sink and trudged up to the allocated treatment area where I emptied it. Min appeared, surprising me, with the water container for the camper and together we made the trek back into the field.

"Thanks for helping."

"I know it was because of breakfast, and I'm glad to help anyway. It's fun. I feel more self-reliant, self-sufficient almost, even though I know we aren't growing vegetables."

"No, but it feels like another world, doesn't it? Electricity from solar, going to laundrettes, hauling water. It's so much to adjust to. I enjoy it, although winter might be different."

"Winter will be very different. If it gets too much, you can always stay with your parents."

I shuddered at the thought, and Min laughed. "Or you could stay with me," she said coyly.

"No, I wouldn't do that. Not yet. Not until the year. And by then I'm hoping I'll know every tip and trick for surviving vanlife in the harsh weather and you'll join me." I regretted mentioning it instantly, as this was the first time anything had been mentioned about what might happen, and I had absolutely no idea if Min had even considered such a life.

"I might have thought about it," she said cryptically.

"And?"

"And we agreed no talk of relationships, remember?"

"You got me there," I laughed.

Once we'd finished our chores and everything was in its place, Anxious insisted we go up to the designated dog field for some exercise. We spent a fun half hour throwing his ball until he'd had enough, then made our way to the security office. We passed a few people on the way, everyone already looking bedraggled and exhausted by the outdoor life. But, as always, fellow festival-goers were friendly, smiled, said hello, or stopped for a chat.

But it was still early, before nine, and most remained fast asleep. I liked this time of day on campsites, and it was even better at the festival. We took a few minutes to explore the stages in the daylight with just a few comatose people laying on benches or sofas at the beer tent, and admired the skill involved building the smaller stages built like tree houses or hidden away down narrow paths. There was even a tunnel you had to crawl through to get into a tiny glade where there was a secret bar I hadn't ever known existed, along with several other cool things we promised we would investigate later.

Having got distracted, it took a while to reach the security cabin, but we found a few men and women on duty but no DS Kate Moss. With a roll of the eyes, and several sniggers, we were informed that she was at the stage overseeing things.

"What's going on? Any trouble?"

"Yeah, all night," said a grizzled and beefy guy who seemed to be in charge. "Poor Moose hardly got a wink as she had him rounding up people and cordoning off the stage. Benny Nails wasn't happy, but she finally let everyone leave, then we were back by seven so she could boss everyone around again."

"Is she still insisting it was an accident?" asked Min.

"Who knows? But I can tell you for certain there's no way that lad managed to stick himself to that bolt then miraculously peel off. It was too high."

"That's what we said," I agreed, warming to the guy. "So you think it was murder?"

"Murder!? Mate, you misunderstood. Whatever happened, it wasn't murder. We were on duty last night and backstage. Nobody stabbed him."

"So how was he killed then?" I asked, nonplussed.

"Beats me," he shrugged. "That's what the police are for, but they don't seem to be doing a very good job of it."

We left them to their tea and went to find DS Moss.

Weaving our way back through to the main stage, it didn't take long to confirm they were there because raised voices rang through the trees. With nobody to stop us, we squeezed between the metal fencing to access backstage, then emerged onto the stage where we found DS Moss staring down Benny Nails. Moose was hanging back, looking uncomfortable, with an officer beside him looking even more stressed out. The crime scene tape had been torn away and was trailing like a party streamer on a welcome gentle breeze.

"Hi," I said brightly.

"You!" DS Moss pointed at me like I'd done something wrong, her tone accusatory.

"Um, yes, it's me," I said, frowning.

"This is your fault."

"What is?"

"Why I spent half the night going over things here and having to deal with this man," she pointed at Benny, "and trying to explain to that man," this time Moose got the finger pointed at him and he stepped back, "why he wasn't to investigate my crime scene."

"We thought you'd wrapped it up?" said Min sweetly. "Didn't you tell us it was a sheared bolt that stabbed Dutch and the case was closed?"

"I didn't say closed. I said it seemed like the bolt was what killed him, but the investigation remained open," she huffed, her neck flushing.

"No, you didn't, ma'am," ventured the officer, wilting under her glare and joining Moose in the shadows.

"Under Mr. Nails' insistence—"

"Call me Benny Nails. Everyone does," he said with a wink to me.

"—I have examined the scene with better lighting and checked for blood along with many other things, and my conclusion is that the offending bolt is not what killed him. The blood spatters don't match, but there was blood on it and it's a health hazard."

"I told you, I'll sort it. It'll take two minutes with an angle grinder."

"Indeed. Every square inch of the stage and surrounding area has been gone over with a fine-toothed comb, but nothing was found apart from coins and empty plastic beer receptacles. Disgusting. People shouldn't litter."

"They pay a pound and re-use them all weekend, but some get dropped when people are dancing. We have teams cleaning up all day long."

"So you say. This place is awful. Why would anyone come here and suffer such basic conditions?"

"Because it's fun?" suggested Min. "A chance to let your hair down, dance, have a drink, meet people, and relax."

"Chance would be a fine thing," sighed DS Moss as she ran her hands through her wavy red hair. I hadn't noticed last night with all the lights, but it truly was fiery red. She was freckled, with incredibly pale skin, and flushed because of the heat and her rising stress levels. Skin like that would not fare well in the crazy temperatures.

"So what's the problem now?" I asked, looking from her to Benny.

"She wants to close down the entire site," he grumbled.

"Would you rather someone else was murdered?" snapped DS Moss.

"Of course not, but you said you had this sorted and knew what happened. Now you're changing your tune. Which is it to be?"

"I'm merely being cautious. My instinct is telling me it wasn't murder, because this place is a death trap. You have sharp metal everywhere, dangerous wiring, and all manner of hazards. After making enquiries, it seems the guitarist, Dutch, jumped into the crowd and may have tripped on stage too. The chance of it being murder is slim to non-existent, but it is there. He died by misadventure, and that's what I will report. Yes, I think we are done here." She wiped her brow with a handkerchief, seemingly now rushing through things so she could leave.

"So now it wasn't murder?" I asked, confused. "First it wasn't, then it was, then it wasn't?"

"I do not appreciate your tone! This is how real detectives work, Mr. Effort. We look at the evidence. It irks me that there is no proof of what killed the victim, but with all the jumping around and the ensuing chaos I doubt we will ever know. You may remove the crime scene tape, officer," she said, beckoning the man forward. "Fix that bolt," she warned, then with a curt nod, she stomped off, her heels clattering on the stage.

"Wow, she's intense," sighed Benny Nails as he rubbed at his large, protruding belly, his slim arms and legs but barrel chest and stomach making it obvious that he was fond of the beer.

"And hard work," said the officer as he untied the tape. He glanced in the direction she'd left, then lowered his voice. "Don't you dare tell her I said that."

"You're secret's safe with us, son," laughed Benny.

"Can I ask you a question?" I asked the officer as he bundled the tape.

"Sure, but I might not be able to answer it."

"First, is she always like that?"

"Always. She's got a thing about dirt and is obsessive about order, but she's a good detective."

"Now for the main question. What does she really think happened?"

"She's convinced the deceased must have been killed by accident. Got caught on something and ripped open his femoral artery. It's one of the wounds that won't stop bleeding, and if the guy didn't notice because he was so hyped up with adrenaline it was just too late by the time anyone could intervene."

"So you agree with her?"

"It's more likely than murder, isn't it? If you were going to kill someone, you wouldn't do it while they were on stage."

"No, but you might while they were crowd-surfing. A little knife, a quick jab in the leg, and it's done. But you're right, the way Dutch was throwing himself about on stage and into the crowd, he would have got plenty of knocks so might not have noticed, especially with the blood running down his leg."

"There you go then. Okay, all done," he said brightly. "Benny Nails, you are officially open for business again, sir."

"Good lad! Thank you, officer." Benny slapped the startled man on the back. "The beers are on me when you're off duty. You're stationed here all weekend, yes?"

"Yes, sir! And I was off duty hours ago. But I'll wait until the evening to take you up on the offer." With a nod, the keen officer left.

"Hi again, Benny." I shook his hand warmly, his firm grip testament to the amount he got involved in getting the festival up and running every year and that he still worked hard even though he gave up farming years ago. With his long, lank hair, slightly puffy features, and tie-dye yellow T-shirt, he was every ounce the raging hippy, although more into the beer than anything more adventurous.

"Great to see you. And especially you, Min. You get prettier every year."

"Thank you. It's lovely to see you too."

They hugged, both having always got on ever since we first starting coming over a decade ago.

"Now, where have you two been the last few years? Max, we didn't get a chance to talk much the other day. I heard a rumour things had turned sour, but if anything it looks like you're both more in love with each other than ever."

"The rumours are true," I admitted. "We're divorced, but still best friends."

"And on your way to re-igniting your love, I can see," he said with a knowing wink. "Come on, it's beer o'clock, so let's go take a load off."

"It's just gone nine in the morning!" laughed Min.

"That late? Blimey, I better get my skates on," said Benny with a crazy wink and a cheeky grin. "Moose, you coming, lad? You deserve a drink after what that woman put you through."

"That's a kind offer, but I'm back at it this afternoon at two, so I better not." Moose considered this for a moment, then declared, "Hell, why not! I was up half the night with the DS, but managed a few hours of sleep, and can have a nap later before work, so yes, I'll have one beer."

"Good lad," said Benny with a deep belly laugh. Nothing could keep him down for long; he was just wired to be happy. "Max, Min, you will, of course, join us?"

"I'll skip the beer."

"I won't," laughed Min.

"Really?" I asked, surprised.

"Why not? When do we ever do anything so crazy? Just a half."

"That's the spirit," said our gracious host as he led the way from the stage. He made a call, asking someone to come and shorten the bolt with an angle grinder, as he hurried towards the beer tent which didn't even open until midday.

Lydstock's owner and founder led us into the tent then disappeared behind the scenes before opening up the bar and sorting out drinks. We then settled around a picnic bench out in the open where he could keep an eye on things.

Crew and volunteers were hard at work clearing rubbish, emptying bins, preparing stages and equipment for the festivities to come, and generally looking happy but busy. Benny watched with satisfaction, having got the festival down to a fine art now after twenty-five years.

He downed half his pint and wiped his mouth with the back of his hand, gasping with pleasure as he said, "Ah, that hit the spot."

Min sipped her beer, I gulped my water, and Moose literally upended his pint into his mouth and it was gone.

When he noted us gawking, he said, "What? I'm a big guy."

"That you are, lad," agreed Benny, slapping him on the back playfully.

"And it's been a long night," sighed Moose, looking utterly worn out.

"Agreed, so let's get down to business," said Benny, turning serious. "Max, I hear you're quite the Columbo these days, and I would like to employ you to discover who murdered poor Dutch."

"Benny, I've already agreed to look into it," I said. "We didn't speak yesterday, but with Dutch being in Uncle Ernie's band, it was only right I'd agree to help in any way I could. Min too."

"Then that's great! That crazy detective gave us the runaround half the night, then had us up at the crack of dawn the moment it was light to check over the scene and ask about a million questions. I assumed she was off her rocker and it was an accident. Nearly wet myself when she kept banging on about the bleedin' bolt. I'd be liable, although the insurance would cover it. But we run a tight ship here, and that was an unfortunate oversight. See, the guys are sorting it now."

We turned to watch a man dealing with the bolt, an angle grinder spitting sparks as he cut it so it wasn't a health hazard.

"And she changed her mind about how Dutch died?" asked Min.

"Yeah, once she got a proper look at the bolt. We all agreed no way he could have been killed by it, and apparently they went over poor Dutch's body properly and it was a small incision made by a flat, sharp instrument. Most likely a small knife as far as I'm concerned. The DS ummed and aahed, but came to the conclusion that it was accidental. How the hell do you get your femoral artery punctured accidentally? I've been around a lot of years, and seen many things, and there's even been the occasional stabbing here. It's inevitable. Now I'm telling you what I told her. It was no accident. But she's made up her mind and that's the end of it as far as she's concerned. So, will you help an ageing hippy out and solve this? I don't want the name of my festival besmirched. It's all I have."

"We'll help in any way we can, Benny. Of course we will."

"Absolutely," agreed Min, smiling warmly as she put her hand over his. "This place means a lot to us, and we know how much work goes into organising and running it. But are you sure it wasn't an accident?"

"I'm sure. Me and the guys went over and over the entire area, checking for anything that could have done this, and there is nothing. Someone murdered poor Dutch, and I want to know who and why. That DS can say what she likes, but she's wrong. She just wants to get out of here, and my guess is she's already filing her report."

"I'll help too," said Moose.

"Thanks, Moose. You've been a fine member of the security team these past few years, and I appreciate that." Benny looked longingly at the bar, but shook his head and sighed. "Guess it's too early for a second pint. Let's catch up later, but if you have any questions you have my number?"

"Sure, still got it," I said. "But before you go. Is there any reason at all that you can think of why someone would kill Dutch like that?"

"It's obvious, isn't it?" he asked with a frown as he stood. "They want to shut me down. It gets worse every year. Not to mention those uppity Third Skatallion guys. Actually, that's not fair, it's mostly Pete, the so-called Major Two-Tone. He's been giving me so much grief for not getting to headline, but I can't let everyone play the prime spot or there wouldn't be a prime spot."

"Pete's been bothering you?" asked Moose. "He's quite intense, isn't he? Is he a real major?"

"No, son, he isn't. It's just a gimmick, but a good one," Benny admitted. "But he isn't happy about missing out on the limelight. They have a good spot this evening before the main act, but even that didn't appease him."

"Ernie reckoned it was him," I said. "But we spoke to the band last night and they said they were together when Dutch was killed."

"It's easy enough to slip away for a few minutes," said Benny. "But my money is on that utter sneak, Campbell.

You know what he's like. He hates that I run a small festival and won't let him take it over and turn it into something obscene."

"He's still after you to sell the rights and let him make it a much larger event?"

"Yeah. He's gone up in the world these last few years. Ever since festivals became properly cool again and numbers keep going up, there's been more and more starting. Any that do well he snaps up. He runs some of the largest ones in the country now, but I refuse to sell. This is my life, what I do, and I like it small and more of a family event. He doesn't let dogs at his festivals, there's not so much for the kids to do, and he even charges for the children. Kids have always come for free and it will stay that way. And what's a festival without a load of dogs? What do you think, Anxious?"

Anxious hopped up into Benny's lap and licked his nose, so we knew what his opinion was on the matter.

Benny laughed, then stroked Anxious as he asked, with tears in his eyes, "Please find who did this. For all our sakes. Once word gets around, and it will, everyone will be freaked out and next year will be a disaster. Save the festival, guys. Save it for all of us. We're a family here. People have been coming for twenty-five years, and everyone knows everyone. We get the youngsters coming and they return time and time again. They came with their parents, now they come with their mates. It's important to everyone." Benny stood again, darted a glance at the beer tent, then nodded, and marched off towards the main stage to check everything was okay.

"We have to solve this, guys," said Moose, eyes dancing with excitement.

"I don't think we have any choice," I said as Min and I exchanged a knowing look.

Anxious barked from my feet. He loved Lydstock as much as anyone. A lot of his friends were here, and he always had the best time ever.

Chapter 7

Moose was keen to get involved, and it was clear he'd be a help the moment we followed him up to the rows of stalls vendors were now opening up. Most were a series of white gazebos provided by Benny, but some had brought their own larger ones if they had the wares to fill them. From clothing to bracelets, stalls consisting of a woman sitting on a chair weaving string into your hair—although I never understood why—to pictures made from recycled magazines and just about all the dream catchers, it was a real hodgepodge of offerings all of which sold well enough for the vendors to come back year on year and tour the country for a living in the summer so they could ride out the leaner months.

Our intrepid security contingent knew them all. Because he was part of the team keeping everyone safe and ensuring disputes over where they could set up were handled professionally and with as little fuss as possible, he was well-respected and quite a character because of his incredible size yet easygoing and mellow manner.

We spoke to everyone we could, asking if there had been any trouble, checking things were running smoothly, enquiring about sales from the first day and generally getting to know everyone. Many were familiar to me and Min already, but in a very casual way as just faces that had been around for years, but there were first-timers, too, and others who had always been rather dour. Here to earn a living, but not into the whole festival scene at all.

After an hour, we were hot, tired, and none the wiser. Resting in the shade, with Anxious thirstily slurping from a bowl of water always topped up for the dogs outside the beer tent that was already attracting quite a crowd of eager people waiting for it to open, we were done with the vendors.

"Sorry I wasn't more help," said a dejected Moose as he hung his head in shame like it was his fault.

"Hey, you did great. You're so nice to everyone, and they like you. If there was anything to find out, I'm sure we would have picked up on something," soothed Min.

"Absolutely," I agreed. "You did great, Moose."

"Really? Thanks, guys. Max, how do you figure these things out?"

"You never stop asking questions, keep your eyes and ears open, and let it percolate. Something will turn up."

"I hope so. Benny's such a great guy, and this place means so much to so many people. I don't want anything to spoil it. Plus, being murdered would suck!" Moose gnawed at his nails, frowning.

Min patted his broad back as we exchanged a look. He was clearly a very sensitive soul, a true gentle giant, and this had hit him hard.

"Hey, what's the matter? Don't get upset," soothed Min.

"It's just... this is such a friendly place. Benny works so hard, all the staff do, everyone has such a great time, and it's the best festival I've ever worked. It's like a family here, with a unique atmosphere, and now a young man's dead and it looks like somebody is out to ruin it for everyone." Moose sniffed into his arm, wiped his round red cheeks, and dried his eyes, then smiled at us sadly. "I'm going to help you find the killer, and we won't let anything stop this festival being the best it's ever been."

"That's the spirit," I said brightly, trying to lighten the mood. Something made me glance around, and I spied Pete, better know as Major Two-Tone, talking to a tall, thin man with dreadlocks hanging past his rear. Both glanced around furtively but didn't spot us because the crowds were gathering, then they exchanged something in their hands and I caught a brief glint of steel.

"Pete just handed that guy a knife," I said. "Don't look now," I warned, "but I'm sure it was. One of those small ones that flip closed."

"Was it a lock knife?" gasped Moose. "They're illegal to carry. You can't have blades that lock open, and you can't carry a folding knife if it's longer than three inches."

"I'm not sure what type it was. I only caught a glimpse. It was small, though, with a wooden inlay. Black and silver metal."

We shifted closer together and adjusted our positions, then turned our heads as one to watch. Pete nodded to the dreadlocked man; he nodded back then spun and walked away.

"I'm going to follow him," said Moose as he rose.

"No, wait, let me," said Min. "He'll spot your uniform, especially with the high-vis jacket, but he won't notice me.

"Min, are you nuts?" I gasped. "He's got a knife. Let Moose do it, or me. It's too dangerous."

"Max is right," said Moose. "But you watch, I'm like a ninja. Nobody sees me once I morph into Ninja Moose." Moose grinned his way out of his jacket, rolled it up, and tucked it into the thigh pocket of his combat trousers. His whole body language somehow changed as he became a different man entirely.

Without waiting for a word from us, he drifted up the slight rise and weaved between people, but whereas before he stomped about like the large man he was, now he was utterly transformed.

"He's like water," gasped Min, our eyes glued to this strange fellow.

"How does he do that? He is like a ninja. That's not even possible. I can hardly even keep my eyes on him."

"Me either. Look at him dodge people and duck behind others then glide across the ground. I swear he keeps going invisible. I can't keep track of him."

"This is some strange stuff happening right here," I whistled, my eyes never leaving Moose but somehow his form was like that of a panther stalking its prey. There but not there. Visible, but impossible to remain focused on.

Only when the hairy man stopped and turned to check behind him, did Moose pause, blending so perfectly with the shadow cast by a gazebo that he became part of it.

"Moose is a ninja," whispered Min.

"Do you think he actually is? How does he do that?"

"I have no idea. But let's focus on Pete, this so-called Major Two-Tone," she said, and we both glanced back to him, but not before I saw the dreadlocked man continue down the track then stop outside a long old bus where he ducked inside. He was the vendor who did the leatherwork. He held demonstrations in the afternoons and you could join in for a nominal fee and he'd show you how to make a belt or a bracelet. His wares were a firm favourite with festival-goers, and many people already sported his high quality offerings.

Moose slid along the side of the bus and peered through a window, somehow managing to blend with the rusty vehicle even though he was twenty plus stone of young meat and muscle who clearly indulged in way too much unhealthy food as he travelled the country helping keep people safe and events organised.

Pete remained rooted to the spot, his eyes in shadow beneath his trilby, but I caught the sly smile that crossed his face before he adjusted his hat then turned and left the beer tent.

He spied us, and was clearly in two minds whether to say hello or not, but he smiled warmly, tipped his hat, and swaggered over.

"Bit early for boozing, isn't it?" he asked brightly.

"I fancied a half, but Max is being a stick in the mud and had water," said Min, patting the seat beside her.

Anxious growled from under the table but didn't take it further once Pete was seated, although he kept a wary eye on him and his tail was still.

"I could do with a drink myself after last night. Terrible thing, right?"

"Awful," I agreed. "You and Uncle Ernie have a lot of history. Sorry if he was unfriendly."

"Unfriendly? That's an understatement, Max. You know me well enough to know I would never murder someone. Your uncle needs his head examining. We may be rivals, but I've always seen it as good-natured competition between fellow music lovers, nothing more."

"Even when you were letting their tyres down at gigs, and phoned venues saying his band couldn't make it and would they like you instead?" I enquired, my eyebrows threatening to leave the top of my head.

Pete laughed, then shook his head as he admitted, "We may have teased him a little. But all in good fun. Just fooling around. Nothing serious or career-ending. Just healthy rivalry and what you get up to when you've been on the road as long as us."

"Sure, Pete, whatever you say."

"Hey now, don't be like that. Yes, there's a little jealousy, and yes, I wanted to headline this year, but I understand. Ernie and Benny Nails go way back, and it was The Skankin' Skeletons turn to shine this year. There'll be other years, other festivals, and soon everyone will see that The Third Skatallion are the best ska punk combo the scene has ever heard. You just wait."

"Pete, you and the guys are great, but give Ernie a break, please?"

"Sure, Max, anything for you. I've always liked you, and it's just messing around. But after what's happened, I promise there will be no more tricks or bickering. So, what's the latest? Was it really murder?"

"The DC says no, we say yes," said Min. "But who knows? Maybe it was a horrid accident."

"Let's hope so. Nobody wants to think there's a murderer knocking off band members. Especially our guitarist. He's freaking out he'll be next this evening. Did you hear? We're playing at eight. Not headlining, but the next best thing. This is our chance to shine. It's gonna blow your uncle's lame show last night out of the water." Pete scowled as he shook his head.

"Hey, I thought you were going to be nice?" I scolded.

"Sorry," he chuckled. "Old habits die hard. But you'll come, won't you? Check us out? Eight on the dot. Don't be late. And we have stunning merch this year. Better than your uncle's duff gear. Proper stuff. We got a good spot too. Usually they make most bands just set up beside the stage after the gig, but that never results in many sales. This year, we have the table right by the track everyone walks up to see the bands, and we can set up for the rest of weekend. Should be a nice earner. Shame your uncle didn't get the same sweet deal."

"I don't even know if he thought much about it," I admitted. "He never said."

"Then he's still a loser. Sorry, I know, we're best friends now!" Pete laughed to himself as he rose, then reminded us again, "Eight o'clock. See what a real ska punk combo sounds like. Plus, we have an incredible show with a lot of drama. After Benny sees this, we'll be headliners next year for sure."

"Okay, Pete, we'll be sure to watch," I agreed, smiling pleasantly at this foul man.

With a grunt, he left.

"I don't like him," hissed Min as we watched him swagger around the festival, talking excitedly to people, laughing and joking. Most likely cajoling everyone to attend their performance this evening.

"Me neither. And I certainly don't trust him. He's oozing resentment, and hates that Ernie got last night's top billing. He could have easily slipped away and stabbed Dutch."

Anxious yipped from under the table, then poked his head out and growled as he sniffed the air, picking up on Pete's noxious scent.

"Yes, Anxious, we don't like him either. Did he do it, boy?" asked Min.

Anxious barked.

"We need to keep an eye on him and make sure he doesn't do anything else to Ernie or the guys," I said. "I have an idea."

"Does it involve food?" asked Min with a wicked grin.

"How did you know?"

"Because you had that dreamy look in your eyes. I know it well."

"A one-pot lunch wonder?" I suggested.

"As long as it doesn't involve sausages or bacon, you can count me in," Min laughed.

"Then I have the perfect thing," I grinned.

"Hey, guys!" said Moose softly.

Min and I both jumped. Anxious barked until he realised it was Moose, then crawled from under the table, up onto the seat, before launching into his arms. Moose cradled him like a tiny teddy bear as his massive forearms rocked Anxious side to side. Within seconds, Anxious was upside down, legs akimbo, tongue lolling, and fast asleep.

"He's a dog whisperer too," gasped Min.

"How on earth did you sneak up on us like that?" I asked, astounded. "We were looking right in your direction.

"Told you, I'm a ninja." Moose kicked out with a heavy boot as his upper body angled sideways until parallel to the floor. His foot was above my head.

"How... What... That's not even a thing, is it?" I spluttered. "Is this even possible? Moose, no offence, but you're a chunky guy, more like a sumo wrestler than the martial arts kick and punch type. You can fight? And flow through crowds like water? How come nobody sees you?"

"Because I will myself invisible and become like water," he shrugged. "As for fighting, I never fight. Don't need to. My bulk sorts out any issues, and I've never had a fistfight in my life. But I could if I wanted to. I watch a lot of videos, and read about the old ways. Secret stuff, like how to trail people without being seen, how to blend in, that kind of thing. I know ancient techniques and even made up a few of my own."

"That's truly astounding," said Min, looking at Moose, just like me, with a renewed level of respect and admiration.

"Thanks," he beamed, back to being regular Moose. He bent his head, whispered something to Anxious, who opened an eye, licked Moose's nose, before sitting and awaiting instructions once he we lowered to the grass. With a quick glance at us, Anxious trotted after Moose as he turned and wandered off.

"Where are they going?" I asked Min.

"No idea. Should we follow? Did he give Anxious instructions and he understood?"

"Looks like it," I said, utterly bewildered. "Come on, let's follow them. Be like water, Min. Be like water," I giggled.

Min tried to be like water, but she was more like a suspicious woman in sexy shorts as she whistled, making herself utterly conspicuous, and kept ducking behind people and stalls as she practised her ninja skills on Moose and Anxious.

"I think you better leave the covert stuff to the professionals," I laughed as I dragged her out of a basket of hats.

"I think you might be the right," she agreed, spitting wool.

Moose and Anxious jumped out from directly in front of the bus, making us squeal. Anxious yipped smugly,

Moose just said, "The leatherworker has gone for an early beer. Come on, I saw where he put it."

"The knife?" I asked.

"Yes, of course. The bus isn't even locked, so let's nip in quick."

"Moose, we can't," I protested. "That's breaking and entering."

"We aren't breaking in. We're just entering. That's not illegal."

"I'm pretty sure it is," I grumbled.

Min shrugged, then "covertly" side-stepped to the door and entered behind Moose.

Anxious looked from me to Min, shrugged, too, and dashed inside.

More concerned about being seen loitering and giving the game away, I reluctantly followed them inside, hoping we wouldn't be caught.

The inside was chaos. Stuff was everywhere. For such a large space, it felt more cramped than Vee, and had zero organisation. The bed was unmade, clothes were strewn on every available surface, and the kitchen area was a health hazard and breeding ground for alien lifeforms judging by the mould in cups and the astonishing number of takeout cartons.

"It reeks in here," complained Min, holding her nose.

"Over here," beckoned Moose, taking up almost the entire width of the bus. "I saw him open a drawer and drop something inside. I bet it's the knife."

We grouped close as Moose pulled open the top drawer of a beat-up pine chest of drawers against a wall. Craning forward, I saw the knife from earlier.

"It was a knife! I knew it!"

"Don't touch it," warned Min. "The DS will want to check for fingerprints."

"Good thinking," said Moose. "Max, this is what you saw?"

"I'm sure of it. A folding blade, and one that locks by the looks of it, so it isn't legal. The same wood, same black detailing. Yes, it's it."

"Every day carry has to be a short blade that doesn't lock," said Moose, "so he wasn't allowed to carry this around. Pete's in a world of trouble now."

"Let's get out of here, and tell the DS," I suggested. "The owner could return at any moment."

We exited quickly, with Anxious already outside keeping an eye out for anyone. Without hanging around, we returned to the security cabin to find DS Kate Moss sitting at a desk, typing on her laptop.

"We have news," I said.

"Not now. I'm finishing my report, then I'm out of this dump." DS Moss held up her left hand for silence while she punched a few keys with her right, then grunted in satisfaction, slammed the lid shut, and turned.

Min explained what we'd discovered, but I could tell immediately that the DS had no interest. When Min had finished recounting her tale, she asked, "Well?"

"Well what? Maybe Pete borrowed it, maybe he wanted this other fellow to look after it. Who knows? And who cares? He had an alibi. I already spoke to him and the other members of his stupid band. I'm not going to spend hours chasing my own tail just to give someone a warning for carrying an illegal knife. And there's no proof anyway. It's in a drawer, so is legal there. You were warned to leave this alone, so get out of my hair and out of my business. My report is filed. This is a done deal."

We left, leaving the poor excuse for a detective to her grumbling and complaining.

Chapter 8

"I guess it's down to us," said Moose happily as he ambled along, nodding to people as we headed to the camping fields.

"Looks that way. I've met quite a few detectives lately, and some are sullen and don't appreciate the public sticking their beaks in, but she's something else."

"Don't be so easy to judge, Max," tutted Moose. "We don't know what's going on in her personal life, or what she's really thinking. Maybe she knows something we don't, or doesn't want us snooping, and that's why she's annoyed."

"True, and you're a wise man, Moose, but I'll bet money on her just not liking it here and wanting to leave. She hasn't investigated properly, if at all, and was quick to blame that sheared bolt."

"But then she spent hours going over everything again and decided it wasn't that. I dunno, but I like to give people the benefit of the doubt when I can."

"You're very sweet," said Min. "Now, I think we can all agree that we need to watch Pete and his band to see if they let anything slip?"

"Sure we do," agreed Moose. "I'm on duty later, so will be there watching them like a hawk."

"And we'll watch them play too. It's looking like it was Pete, but we need more information. Clues. Something to prove his guilt."

"We'll find what we need," said Moose, about as chipper as a man could be.

"What are you so happy about?" I asked, smiling at our new friend.

"I'm stoked you let me in on this investigation. Security isn't as glamorous as you might think, and it's mostly just wandering around and organising stuff, but this is the real deal. You two are the real deal. It's fun, but in a sad way."

"We're pleased to have your help. So far, you've done great, and uncovered the only clue, so well done," said Min.

Moose beamed with pride and his chest swelled as he walked ahead, a skip in his step.

"Moose, do you want to come for lunch at ours?" I asked after receiving a nod from Min that I should invite him.

Moose stopped dead and spun, causing us to jump back and Anxious to sniff the air suspiciously. "You mean it?"

"Of course. It would be great to have you. We can relax for a while, and we're going to invite The Skankin' Skeletons. They're playing later, but will want food first."

"I get to hang with you guys and a famous band? Yes please," he gushed.

"Then find us in an hour or so. Make that two. Get some rest, then come for lunch."

"I can't wait."

Something changed, the air charged with a peculiar energy, and Moose went rigid.

"What's wrong?" asked Min.

"Clown," he hissed, shivering.

"Clown?" I asked, exchanging a concerned glance with Min.

"Clown," he agreed. "I can smell them a mile off."

"Hi," beamed a clown as he jumped out from behind a tree, a gaggle of children screaming and running towards us as they spied him.

"Hi. You normally surprise people like that?" I asked, nonplussed.

"Um, yeah, quite often," laughed the clown, his heavy make-up making it impossible to not think of all the horror movies I'd watched over the years once Min went to bed as she was as much a fan as Moose clearly was. "Sorry, I was just taking a breather from the kids. They run me ragged."

"No problem," I said. "I like your style. Very understated."

"Thanks! I'm experimenting. Heavy on the smile and the big red nose, but I've toned the rest down," he said, oblivious to my teasing sarcasm.

"Bet you don't get a minute to yourself, do you? You're here every year, right?"

"Oh yes. Been coming for donkey's years. Ever since I was a kid I always enjoyed the circus, so used to volunteer and help out." He turned to Min and smiled, then said, "Hello, would you like to smell my flower?" Waggling his heavily painted eyebrows, he tugged at the plastic yellow flower in his huge lapel.

"No way. I'm not falling for that! You'll squirt water at me."

"Fair enough," he shrugged.

"And I've seen you around," he said to Moose, extending his hand.

Woodenly, Moose thrust his hand out and shook, then jumped back, choking down a wail as he looked at the exposed buzzer in the clown's hand.

"Sorry, couldn't resist," he laughed. Glancing at the approaching horde, he added, "Well, gotta go," and skipped off backwards, waving his hands at the children.

"I hate clowns," grumbled Moose, shaking out his hand.

"They freak me right out," agreed Min. "You never know what the person really looks like, and they always seem about to pull out an axe and say something terrifying."

Anxious growled his agreement, and rubbed against my leg for comfort.

"They're funny," I chortled. "The children love them. And this guy is always around. He teaches them juggling, shows them how to dress up, how to do a pratfall without hurting yourself. Just good fun."

"Never trust a man who has a permanent smile," said Moose solemnly.

We watched the children racing after him, the clown throwing glitter at them then stumbling on purpose so they could pounce.

"I gotta go," said Moose. "But I'll be over for lunch later."

After explaining where we were camped, we left Moose to get some much-needed rest and returned to Vee.

Anxious, tired from the excitement and close to overheating, set up camp under Vee and promptly crashed out. I felt like doing the same, but got lunch prepped in record time, put the cast-iron pot on to simmer, then joined Min in the shade and collapsed into my chair.

"I'm wiped out," I complained.

"Me too. You should have let me help with lunch."

"You did breakfast," I said with a wink, "so now it's my turn. Moose is a dark horse, isn't he?"

"He's incredible. How does he do it?"

"I'm guessing he's practised a lot. Maybe he is a ninja."

Min laughed, then said, "You don't really get ninjas, Max. Don't be silly. But he definitely has the moves."

I was already half dreaming, and was soon drifting off listening to people chatter and play music as kids ran around, dogs barked, and the world felt surprisingly dreamlike and peaceful despite the noise. Before I knew it, I was fast asleep.

Waking to the amused smile of Min with a backdrop of blue sky and green grass, plus a sea of tents, was the best wake-up call I'd ever had. The day felt like a lazy Sunday afternoon in the garden, but as the sounds filtered in and racy guitar riffs echoed from the arena, I slowly came back to the present and remembered where we were.

"Hey there, sleepyhead. Time to rise and shine," beamed Min, eyes twinkling.

"Wow, I crashed right out," I yawned. "Did you sleep?"

"A little, but I slept well last night. Feel better for an hour of kip?"

"Much. Did you check on lunch?" I asked in a panic, surging to my feet.

"It's taken care of. Relax," she soothed, grinning at me.

"What's so funny?"

"You stressing about lunch. Some things will never change, will they?"

"If I buy ingredients, and we're going to eat meat and vegetables, then they deserve respect. It's only fair they are given due attention and their true beauty allowed to shine through."

"Here we go again," teased Min.

"Hey, that's not fair," I protested, edging over to the pot. "You can make the simplest of ingredients become something wonderful if you treat them right. You know that. I like to do that whenever possible. I may not prepare fancy meals anymore, and back-to-basics cooking might not be Michelin star-worthy to some, but for me it's even more important. It's how it should have always been. I enjoy cooking, so I don't want to let the producers, or the fact an animal lost its life, be for nothing."

"I was only teasing. I think it's admirable, and you are right. Shame we can't say the same about my fry-ups."

"Most of what you cook is delicious. Everyone has the occasional issue."

"Apart from you." Min pointed an accusing finger at me, but she was only teasing.

I merely shrugged, beaming at her, then lifted the lid of the pot and sniffed. It smelled incredible, and was about done, so after a drink of water and a quick wash in the bowl we'd kept for just that, I sorted out a few things. Min helped set out cutlery and bowls, sliced the bread, and laid everything on a blanket for when everyone arrived, then we settled into our chairs and had a cheeky celebratory glass of Prosecco.

"What are we celebrating again?" she asked as she sipped and giggled because the bubbles went up her nose. Something she always did.

I shrugged. "Being alive. Eating good food. Having the best company ever. All of it. Chilling at festivals, listening to music, playing with Anxious. Speaking of which. Where is he?"

"Still under the van. Poor thing isn't coping with the heat too well."

"Ah, that reminds me. It only came yesterday morning, and I wanted to wait until he really needed it. What with one thing and another, I forgot. He's always handled the heat, but this is too intense even for him now. You must have seen it?"

"Seen what?"

"Give me a moment." I popped into the van, retrieved the surprise, then returned to Min.

Anxious knew something was up, so appeared, then sat and waited while I removed the item.

"Apparently, you dunk it in cold water, wring it out, and it works like magic." I followed the instructions, using water I'd put in a bowl in the coolbox, then showed them.

"What is it?" asked Min.

"It's a cool vest for dogs."

"It doesn't look that cool. I mean, the colours are nice, but the last thing he needs is clothes. That'll make him hotter."

"No, it's got all these layers and a special mesh. The water is stored in the middle layers but won't make Anxious wet. Somehow, it draws out heat and evaporates. Lots of people use them. We should give it a try."

"I wondered why dogs were wearing jackets in this weather. That's clever."

Anxious came over and sniffed the vest, and once satisfied it posed no threat, I slid it on then fastened the buckles under his belly. He stood stock still for several seconds, then shivered and shook himself out. The vest stayed put, which was a good start.

"He looks very cute," giggled Min. "You look smart, Anxious. Is it working?"

"I don't think it is. That's a shame."

Anxious sat and pondered things in his own imitable way, then came to a decision. He jumped up, ran around us, then yipped as he tore off across the field and sprinted right to the other end. He was back in seconds flat, panting happily.

"I think we can agree it's working," I laughed. Anxious sidled up to me and I placed my palm on the vest. It was cold to the touch and damp, but not soaking. Easing my hand under it onto his fur, I was shocked to find that he was dry, but nice and cool. "Wow, that's incredible. He's frosty."

"Maybe we need one each," said Min. "I'm burning up."

"Maybe put your bikini on?" I suggested innocently.

"We have guests coming, and you're hot enough already," she teased.

"Not as hot as you."

"Sort out lunch," Min ordered. "I can see Ernie and the guys, and I think that's Moose behind them."

"Did someone say my name?" asked Moose as he stepped out from behind the van.

Min, Anxious, and I gasped.

"That is not possible," said Min. "Moose, was that you halfway up the field a moment ago?"

"You must be mistaken," he smirked, tugging at his black polo shirt coyly.

"And Anxious didn't even get your scent," I said in wonder.

Anxious trotted over and sat in front of Moose, tail wagging happily, enjoying this fun game he had with our new friend.

Moose snapped his fingers and the next thing we knew, Anxious was in his arms and being rocked.

"No way!" I blurted. "Min, did you see Anxious jump?"

"No, I didn't. Moose, who are you?"

"Just a regular security guy," he said, nonplussed. "Anxious feels nice. I see you got him one of those cool vests."

"He seems to like it, and it's definitely working."

"And here I am in my boots and dark trousers and shirt. I have work straight after lunch, so figured I'd get ready. It's so hot though."

"Prepare to get even hotter," I teased, "because lunch will be ready in five."

"Can't wait. Thanks again for inviting me."

"It's our pleasure, Moose. Have a seat. Um, I'm not sure you'll fit on the chairs though. They aren't made for big men like you."

"That's okay. I'll sit on the blanket." Moose lowered Anxious, who looked dazed by Moose's strange ways, then he sat without issue, when I'd expected him to struggle because of his weight. He was very agile, and I felt bad for judging him, but he moved with an ease and grace that I had never seen before.

Ernie and some of the guys arrived a moment later, keen to chat and even more keen to eat. Chaos Charlie, Sizzling' Stu, and Doc Crocs had joined him, but the others were either resting, or had said they couldn't face eating anything hot, although Ernie explained it was mostly nerves. Even after all these years, and having brought the house down yesterday, the others still got jittery before a gig, even a more low-key affair like they had this afternoon.

"Don't you ever get nervous, Ernie?" asked Min.

"Me? Of course! My stomach's churning and I'm sweaty, and not from the heat, but that's part of it. Once you get up there, and the adrenaline kicks in, you forget all that and just have a skankin' good time.

"I'm the same," admitted Doc Crocs. "Still have the nerves, but it's always worth it. And today we owe it to poor Dutch to get up there and show everyone we won't be scared off."

There were mumbles of agreement, then I realised I hadn't made introductions.

"Everyone, this is Moose. Moose, this is—"

"We all know Moose," said Charlie. "We see him everywhere we go. How you doing, Moose?"

"Fine, thanks, Charlie. Sorry about what happened. I know I saw you last night, but it was a chaotic time. I'm helping Max and Min solve it, and we seem to be getting somewhere."

"Really?" asked Charlie, intrigued.

"Yes, and you won't believe it," he said sheepishly.

We filled them in on what we'd learned, which wasn't much beyond what we'd seen Pete do with the knife, but also spent a few minutes regaling them with how dismissive the DS was.

"So that's it?" asked Ernie. "It really was Pete? I'll wring his neck! How could he do something like this? I know we have our differences, but murder?"

"Ernie, you can't say a word. Nobody can," I said. "Yes, it looks bad, and yes, he's a slippery one, but we need more proof. The DS won't do a thing, and unless we get more evidence he's going to get away with it. But I can tell you one thing for sure. Just because it seems like he's guilty doesn't mean he is. Pete might be involved, or could have asked the leatherworker to hide the knife for someone else, or any number of reasons, so we need to keep cool heads and watch our backs. That goes for everyone now, okay? No trying to get justice yourselves. If you hurt Pete then we discover it was someone else, you could go to jail and the killer might get away with this. Understand?"

"Max, you know more about these things than us," said Ernie, "so we promise not to do anything. But I know it was that snake, same as we all do."

The other band members murmured their agreement, but I had other ideas. I didn't have that tingle, that sense of certainty, so I withheld my judgement even though there was clearly something going on with Pete and the knife.

"Now, let's eat!" I declared to a round of applause.

It took the two of us to haul over the cast-iron pot. It was full to the brim and I was still panicking it wouldn't be enough, especially with a large guy like Moose. Everyone leaned forward as we placed the pot on the wooden chopping board in the centre of the blanket, then I rather dramatically lifted off the lid with an oven glove and we were enveloped in a cloud of steam, the spicy aromas intense. I knew it would be delicious.

With murmurs of appreciation and eager anticipation, I dished up the one-pot jerk chicken and rice dish, giving everyone a healthy portion, surprised to discover there was actually a little left.

Once our guests were settled, and with Anxious waiting impatiently for his, I placed a bowl before him with the chicken already taken off the bone as cooked bones were dangerous for dogs, especially small ones, then with all eyes on me, I declared "Tuck in!"

Nobody needed telling twice, and we ate with gusto, our worries and concerns forgotten for a while as we enjoyed good food, great company, and pleasant conversation. Unsurprisingly, Anxious was the first to finish, then returned to guilt everyone into giving him more even though he wasn't meant to have lunch at all. Once he was asked to behave, he lay down, cool and happy with a full tummy and his new vest bulging at the waist.

"How do you do this?" asked Moose as he ate slowly, his cheeks red and his smile as wide as everyone else's.

"It's what I do," I shrugged. "I've always been methodical and like to ensure I get everything just right."

"Obsessive, you mean," laughed Min.

"Yes, I guess."

"Oh, Max, I didn't mean that in a bad way. Not now, anyway. Moose, Max has always had a keen eye for detail. In his cooking, and in everything. He notices the small things and it makes a difference."

"How'd you mean?"

"Say for instance some people might go by a recipe and follow it perfectly. The end result is that the meal tastes good, but not incredible. Max will adjust as he goes. Tasting, changing the heat, removing something if it's cooking quicker than everything else, or adding more spices or salt. Whatever it takes to get it just so. He can taste a dish and know what ingredients were used, and mimic it perfectly, if not make it better."

"Thank you," I told Min, pleased she wasn't making my rather single-track mind a negative. "So today I figured some real festival food like the vendors offer would go down a treat. Something spicy but not too crazy hot. Simple, but full of flavour. Did I pull it off?" I asked, knowing I had.

"Yes!" everyone roared through a mouthful of chicken and rice.

Beaming, I thanked them, and we finished our meal.

Ernie and the guys offered to help clean up, but I could see the nerves were rising and they were beginning to get antsy at not having enough time to prepare for their set, so we shooed them off and promised to come watch in an hour when they began.

Moose hung around helping, and was clearly an old hand at the outdoor life. He instinctively knew where to put things, how best to organise everything, and in short order we were done, no sign of seven people having just eaten.

While Anxious dozed, Moose said farewell, and we promised to meet up with him later to discuss things and see if anyone had any new information on what was turning out to be a very confounding mystery.

"So, what now?" asked Min.

"Now we go listen to some music, enjoy the day, and see what happens. We are here to have fun, right?"

"Absolutely! And I even brought my festival hat."

I groaned as Min skipped to her car and rummaged around. She was a woman of fine sensibilities and understated but undeniable style, and always looked incredible, but her taste in hats was downright peculiar.

Chapter 9

"What do you think?" Min spun, her tanned legs tasty, her trim body jaw-dropping, bouncy hair glistening in the sunlight. This sweet woman's face was beautiful, with a smile to die for. Her hat was a blood-curdling crime against fashion and it hurt my eyes to look at it.

Anxious groaned from the sun shelter and put his paws over his head; he'd been here before and always walked a few steps behind her when others might see.

"Um, it's your festival hat," I said magnanimously. "It's as bright and tall and memorable as always." I winked at Anxious as he risked a peek, and mouthed a silent, "Be nice."

"Thanks! I love my festival hat. It's just so shiny."

"It is very shiny," I agreed. "That'll be all the sequins and ribbons you sewed on, and the rainbow colours, and the pom-pom."

"I did put a lot of work into it," she declared happily. "Took me ages. It's not too, um, bright?"

"Not as bright as the sun," I said solemnly, squinting as harsh light bounced off the sequins and I feared she'd incinerate the campsite if she stayed in one spot for too long and let the rays focus.

Min's smile faltered and her shoulders dropped as she tugged at her lip. "Too much?"

"Min, you look beautiful. It's fun, you love it, and this is a music festival. Anything goes. Honestly, you are radiant!"

"Oh, thank you! I do love it, but for a minute I thought you were making fun of me and I looked like a muppet."

"You could never look like a muppet. I think you look stunning whatever you wear, or don't wear."

"In your dreams, mister." Min smiled happily, then called for Anxious. We locked up then headed back into the thick of things.

The festival was now in full swing, with several stages drawing large crowds. Performers were doing everything from acrobatics to stilt walking to juggling, showcasing incredible costumes and having as much fun as everyone else. The atmosphere was buzzing.

We crawled through a bizarre tunnel made of tin sheeting and emerged into a clearing where a bar had been set up and an acoustic trio provided mellow tunes for folks to unwind to. We sampled a cocktail called Benny's Brain Bender, which probably wasn't such a smart idea as we both felt decidedly weird halfway through drinking it and figured we'd better switch to soft drinks. Whatever was in it, it was fast to come and fast to go, so after chilling for a while we were re-energised.

Next, we caught the last few songs of an up-and-coming hip-hop metal combo that went down a storm, and even Anxious had a little dance amongst the accommodating small crowd amassed in front of the cramped stage. He got plenty of warm smiles and doting pats because he looked so cute with his cool vest and earmuffs.

During the interlude, Ernie and the others set up their stand, which was how most bands made their money. Gigging was the bread and butter for the majority of acts, earning their living from ticket sales but more importantly the merchandising where they got to keep most of the money.

It was a fast turnover, so while they were laying out T-shirts, hoodies, CDs because they were old school, or QR codes on fancy artwork people could scan to download albums or songs, the previous band was doing a brisk business beside them.

People were happy to part with their money at such events, as it was part of the reason why they came, and understood that if they wanted festivals like this to continue it had to be worth the acts' time.

Ernie had confided in me that the takings from the previous evening had been incredible. Even after the untimely demise of Dutch, sales had continued as nobody had been aware of it, so with the stand being off to one side earnings had been the best ever. He lamented not being able to nab a prime spot like The Third Skatallion had, one where they could keep their offerings on display for the whole event, but that was the trade-off he'd agree with Benny Nails for headlining and to placate Pete and his crew so they would come and play.

This was an event deeply rooted in ska and reggae even though it had morphed over the years to include more rock, heavy metal, and even drum and bass DJs. The latter caused its popularity to rise because the younger crowd began to come, but at its heart there were still numerous old rockers who liked the more mellow sounds of previous decades. Benny Nails had to run the event in such a way that kept everyone happy. No mean feat, but so far it had worked and continued to do so, with an eclectic mix of music and people with one thing in common.

Having fun, supporting talented musicians, and getting away from the madness that continued at a frenetic pace the other side of a few fields.

Soon enough, The Skankin' Skeletons were announced and they took to the stage. They were in their usual skeleton make-up and looked as awesome as ever, but there was something missing, and it was obvious what. No Dutch. Ernie had taken over as guitarist, but it meant he couldn't jump around and perform like usual, and although the set was undoubtedly top-notch and everyone had a fun time, singing along to classics, going wild over some catchy new songs, and they finished on a real high, I could tell that Ernie and the others weren't on usual form and it was certainly nothing like the previous night's headline gig. Ernie was a good guitar player, but nowhere near up to Dutch's standards, and at times the upbeat vibe was lost as he had to focus on his playing rather than his performing.

It was to be expected, and this was meant to be an altogether more low-key affair, with more light ska and less of the heavy punk tracks, but they were still rather sedate even for this type of appearance.

Maybe it was just me, though, as the crowd applauded wildly, the lighting engineers did themselves and The Skankin' Skeletons proud, and the moment the band finished people flocked to the merchandise stall where a pretty young girl—a volunteer who got to enjoy the festival for free in exchange for a few hours of work every day—smiled warmly and took people's money.

As usual, the band converged to help out, talk to fans, and sign whatever was put in front of them. We hung back, waiting for the crowd to disperse before the next act began, so once sales dried up we went over to help pack everything away.

"That was great!" said Min, hugging Ernie then the others. "Well done."

"Thanks, but it didn't feel the same," said Ernie. "I know Dutch was only a stand-in, but he was one of us and it wasn't right without him."

"You did really well," said Doc Crocs, slapping Ernie on the back. The others murmured their agreement.

"I was alright, but I couldn't give my performance the oomph it needed," sighed Ernie, his make-up running.

"It was meant to be a mellow set anyway," said Sizzlin' Steve. "We did good. And we proved that nothing will stop us. Don't be so hard on yourself, Ernie. You were a star, same as always."

They all agreed he did very well, and although they were being supportive, it was clear there was a cloud over all of them. Everyone was antsy and jumpy, and we all knew why.

"To be honest," said Skully, still clutching his drum sticks, "I'm just glad nobody was murdered. I didn't say anything to you guys, but all the way through I was kinda stressing I was gonna get shanked. I was a right bag of nerves."

"Me too!" gasped Doc Crocs.

Everyone else agreed, relieved to discover they weren't the only one who was concerned.

"You men!" tutted Min. "Why didn't you talk to each other about it? Of course you would be worried. Your friend was killed. You should have spoken up."

"Min's right, we should have," said Ernie, smiling at her. "Min, you are a wise woman, and I love your hat."

"Thanks," said Min with a wink at me as she toyed with a ribbon dangling in front of her flushed face.

"At least we had Moose and his guys watching our backs," said Ernie as he spied Moose weaving through the crowd waiting for the next act.

"Hey," said Moose. "Good set."

"Thanks," said Ernie. "No trouble?"

"No trouble," Moose confirmed. "We had people backstage, and I was out front by the engineers' booth watching everyone. Nobody looked suspicious, nobody acted stranger than you'd expect, and it was all good."

"That's a relief. Thanks, Moose. Right, I need to shower and change, then it's time to party!" roared Ernie.

"Party!" the others screamed.

With a nod, Ernie and the guys left.

"They need to de-stress," noted Moose.

"They sure do. They did amazingly well to carry on today. They're hurting over Dutch."

"But the show must go on," said Moose. "And they're professionals."

"They really are," I said, feeling very proud of my uncle. "Any news?"

"Nothing yet, but I'm keeping my eyes and ears open." Moose pushed his ears forward and smiled cheerily.

"So are we. Maybe this was an unfortunate accident like the DS insisted?" mused Min.

"Do you really think that?" I asked.

"No, but I wish it was just a terrible accident."

"I've seen Pete a few times, wandering around like he owns the place and bragging about his prime spot for merchandise. Have you seen it yet? They weren't allowed to set up until today because that wouldn't have been fair on Ernie and the others, but they've really gone for it."

"No, we haven't seen. What's it like?"

"Come and see. A few bands have got the best tables and they're arguing over stuff and making a right song and dance."

Moose led the way, so we followed, the crowds making the going slow now the afternoon was here and everyone was in the mood to party.

After weaving around a very keen sword swallower, ducking under a limbo pole—Anxious nailed it—sidestepping another terrifying clown because they all are, and giving a woman with a flaming hula hoop a very wide berth as she spat flames from her mouth, we eventually made it onto the thoroughfare to the main stage. Lined up along the fence or on the opposite side of the well-trodden path were tables and marquees rammed with band merchandise.

Most had proper tablecloths and banners, whilst a few had more intricate and expensive props, but they were all busy and this was definitely where the money was at.

"Why didn't Ernie get a place here?" asked Min.

"Because they got the headline gig. Benny said as there were only a few tables available, he thought it fair to let Pete's lot have a permanent one. Seems weird, but he's trying to be fair and is thinking about the future. Ernie gets a better spot next year, The Third Skatallion don't."

"But the other headline acts have a permanent table."

"I know, but I guess over the years they've had to miss out, same as Ernie. It must work out somehow. Pete and his guys will earn good money from sales, but Ernie and his band will have been paid much more for headlining. It's swings and roundabouts."

"And will you look at them bickering?" Moose drew our attention to the packed booths, the staff and band members in each other's faces, arguing over where T-shirts were hung or how much space there was between each table. They were trying to keep it away from the customers, but were putting people off even if they were whisper shouting.

An aged rocker with long hair and purple sunglasses swung a punch at a young, rising reggae star, who ducked, then clobbered him with a vinyl record before jumping on the overweight man and slapping his face with a Jamaican flag. It took two security guards to pull them apart.

"Benny needs to have a re-think about how he handles this," grumbled Moose. "It's caused more trouble than anything."

"The Third Skatallion seem to be doing alright," I noted. They had a spot at the end of the walkway before you got to the main stage, so everyone would see them while they watched the acts, and the whole band were busy taking orders.

"They're making a killing," said Moose. "Mind you, it isn't cheap to get stuff printed, so there's not much profit per item. But it adds up."

"How do you know?" I asked.

"Because people talk, and I listen," he shrugged.

We wandered over to The Third Skatallion's stall and admired the clothing. It was top quality and the branding was excellent. They played on the military theme, with a lot of greens and browns then silhouettes of the band or Major Two-Tone in his black and white faux army gear, along with other cool logos and whatnot. People were buying in droves, even though they were yet to play.

"Doing well, Pete?" I asked.

"Amazing!" he gushed. "I'll take this over a headline gig any day," he laughed, but it was short-lived and too forced. He was still angry at missing out, and a prideful man, so no way would he prefer selling more T-shirts to having top billing.

We left them to it and walked slowly up to the beer tent. I paused when I noted Doc Crocs leaning against a food stall and peering out, watching Pete closely, a deep scowl on his face. What was he doing? Why was he watching like that? Maybe he expected Pete to show his true colours and somehow reveal his guilt? Very unlikely, but I didn't interfere.

Moose had his duties, so we said goodbye and spent the rest of the afternoon lazing around on a blanket with intermittent trips for snacks and drinks. Anxious was happy to sleep when he could, but as always at festivals the true stars of the show were dogs, so a near-constant stream of people came to say hello and asked if they could stroke him. Children loved his new vest, and word soon got around that there was a cool—literally—dog that you could stroke if you got too hot, so we made plenty of new friends and as the day wore on Anxious got fatter and fatter as the kids loved feeding him.

We danced to a few bands, we ran for the shade many times, and we drank slightly too much, but not so much that we overdid it. Just a few drinks interspersed with lots of water and fizzy pop to keep our sugar levels high enough to jump around when the mood took us.

By dinnertime we were hot and sweaty, tired but amped, and looking forward to a full evening of more of the same. We decided to freshen up at the nearest sink, so after a quick wash and dab of deodorant, we returned to the packed arena and joined queues for food. We went for a simple pizza done in a portable wood-fired oven and it was incredible. Puffy crust, a hint of basil, and plenty of cheese, with charred edges and a soft middle.

Ernie made an appearance with the guys, so we settled on blankets with some drinks and soaked up the atmosphere.

"What's the truth about the stalls?" I asked him.

"Ah, that," he said sourly. "It's a bit of a bone of contention. Benny Nails wanted us to have the best location the whole weekend, but Pete kicked up a fuss and insisted he got a permanent table too. Benny relented because Pete said they might not play at all if they had no headline spot and no prime real estate."

"So you missed out?"

"We still did well last night and today, but yes, it could have been better. But we got paid really well, so it's still a winner for us. Next year we'll get the best stand, but no headline gig, so it works out."

"Some of the others selling their gear aren't headliners, though, are they? What about the old rockers? They get top billing every Sunday, don't they? And a great location to showcase their stock."

"Benny's trying to bring in a younger crowd, so things change, but Danger to Life are stalwarts and everyone loves them. Apparently, they threatened to boycott, too, just like Pete, but the difference being if the old-timers didn't come Benny would have lost about a quarter of ticket sales."

"They're that popular?"

"Oh yeah. Max, they're one of the first bands to ever play here. They did it as a favour to Benny as they were already huge, but on the wane. It's what made this festival. They come most years, and always play an incredible set. They're a band with followers who go everywhere they go, and it's a large, dedicated crowd."

"And they threatened to pull out if they didn't get a good location?"

"Yep, same as Pete. I'd never do that. It's not fair to Benny. He does his best to appease everyone, but if too many bands are selling their gear sales are low for everyone. Most bands just get to set up while they play, like we did, which works well anyway as people buy on impulse as they know it's their only opportunity. Why are you asking?"

"Just curious. Trying to figure out how things work. When are Danger to Life playing? I've seen them so many times, but I do like them. Proper old rock band."

"They're the headline act at about nine tomorrow, I think. They're good guys, but a little up themselves. Been on the scene longer than me, if you can believe it!" he laughed. "They used to play huge stadiums back in the day, and sell millions of records. They still act like they're doing that, but I guess that's fair enough. I suppose it would rankle to be doing the small festival circuit after that. Me, I'm just happy to be playing."

"And having the headline gig?" I teased.

"Yeah," he agreed with a belly laugh, "and getting the headline gig."

Soon enough it was time for The Third Skatallion to take to the stage. This was going to be interesting.

Chapter 10

Anxious was getting antsy because of his vest as the sun sank behind the hills, so I removed it and left it with our pile of stuff but put on his earmuffs so he could enjoy the fun without it stressing him out.

We joined Ernie and the guys to the side of the engineers' booth again, affording us a great view without getting too caught up in the chaos that was sure to ensue once The Third Skatallion got going.

The crowd was large, surprisingly so, and I wondered if word had spread about Dutch and part of this was morbid curiosity to see if anything else would happen. The police and security were clearly taking no chances, and had an impressive presence around the arena, with Moose and his fellow security guards to the side of the stage and at the railings separating people from the acts.

Min and I exchanged a worried look, both clearly having the same idea.

"Do you think something will happen?" we both asked.

Laughing, we both agreed it was unlikely, but with no motive for Dutch's death, and only a suspicion it was Pete, we were truly at a loss.

The lights dimmed, then went out completely, leaving the haze of dusk. A lone bugle sounded, crisp and clear like a forewarning of the battle to come. But this was to be no battle of soldiers, it was a battle of ska, and The Third Skatallion intended to take no prisoners.

With a boom of a bass guitar, and the *rat-tat-tat* of staccato drumming vibrating the ground, the stage erupted in a cacophony of sound and light as fireworks went off and the smoke machine belched its contents into the crowd.

And they were off!

Straight into the unmistakable rhythm of ska, everyone cheered and danced for all they were worth as Major Two-Tone belted out short, snappy lyrics to the beat before the trumpet kicked in, the guitar pounded, and the sax overlaid everything in perfect time.

The band were on fire! With their matching black and white military style garb, artful camouflage painted faces, and green trilbies, they looked incredible and sounded even better. There was no denying they were up there with the best, even The Skankin' Skeletons, though it pained me to admit it.

Min was bopping along beside me, a guilty look on her face as she glanced at Ernie, but he was mesmerised, studying everything with a keen eye, just like his bandmates.

The applause was infectious as the song ended, and Pete introduced himself and the band, all with faux military names, before they jumped straight into one of their classics, the lighting timed to perfection, the angry guitar giving a real edge to a ska punk combo track that had always got the crowd going. Tonight was no exception, and they played like things possessed. As though they had something to prove to themselves, to Benny Nails, and to the crowd.

Track after track was performed perfectly, timing incredible, the atmosphere charged and getting wilder as they increased the tempo and the lyrics became angry then mellow, inviting then aggressive, flowing around us, carrying us up and down with a tidal wave of pure emotion.

"They're bloody good," admitted Uncle Ernie through gritted teeth.

"They are. Not as good as you, but they sure can put on a show," I agreed.

"Shame. I was hoping they'd blow it." Ernie watched for a while longer, then left with a few of the others, while the rest dispersed into the crowd to get a closer look.

Min and I stayed put, enjoying ourselves despite our mistrust of Pete.

The last track finally ended and the band came forward and bowed as the spotlights hit them.

"Encore!" everyone shouted.

Major Two-Tone doffed his hat, pointed his swagger stick at the crowd, raised the mike, and shouted, "Are you ready to skank until you can't skank no more?"

"Yes!" they roared.

The bugle sounded once more, ringing out as the entire festival was silent for a moment, then the jagged riffs of the guitar began and all hell broke loose. Wild, frenzied, faster and faster, the song was frenetic and Pete's vocals were raw and angry, spitting out lyrics like he was battling for his life.

And then, with perfect timing, the track ended as the lights stuttered then turned blood red.

Major Two-Tone flung his arms wide, beamed at the crowd, and tipped his head back and laughed as he basked in the crowd's glory.

Something glinted as it crossed the arena, sparkling as it caught the spotlights tracing over everyone.

Even from our vantage point, I heard the dull thwack and began running forward as Major Two-Tone's white polo shirt burst into life as a crimson flower bloomed. He looked down at the arrow sticking from his chest, grunted, then grinned as he whispered, "What a way to go," his words caught by the mike still in his hand. Finally, he toppled backwards slowly, arms still wide. Dust billowed as he slammed into the stage; his legs twitched once, then he was still.

The curtains closed, and for one person they would never open again.

For a moment that seemed to last an eternity, the entire festival fell silent, then the screams began.

Trying to get to the stage, I was engulfed in a stampede of people and had no choice but to retreat to Min and Anxious who were pinned up against the engineers' booth. I scooped up the trembling Terrier and soothed him, then we circled around to the back out of the way and waited until the screams died down and people stopped running. Everyone laughed, thinking they'd been duped, believing it was part of the act.

"You okay?" I asked Min.

"Fine. Did you see anything?"

"Only the arrow flying over everyone, then Pete dying very dramatically."

"Max, don't be so heartless!"

"I wasn't being heartless. He did die dramatically. He had real flair, I'll give him that. Nobody's going to forget that in a hurry."

"I think we can rule him out as a suspect, don't you?"

"Absolutely. But who would do something like this? Did you see anyone? How can you use a bow and arrow and not be seen?"

"There are lots of dark places. All the stalls, the stands rammed with T-shirts, even here by the engineers. The lights are so bright, then so dull, and they're shining this way and that. It's impossible to keep track of anything. They could have been anywhere."

"Have you seen Ernie or the others?"

"Not since they left. Do you think he's in danger?"

"I don't know. But I'd like to know where they are. These guys hate each other and now it's a band member each that's dead. Something is seriously up with this whole picture and it's becoming too dangerous to be around any of them."

"You don't think Ernie..."

"No, he wouldn't kill Pete however much he disliked him."

"I had to ask. But of course you're right. He's such a sweetie. What about the others? Maybe for retribution? We all knew about the knife, so maybe it was a revenge killing?"

"Maybe it was. I'm going to go down and see what I can do to help. But let's get you both somewhere safe first."

"No!" Min stamped her foot and locked her resolute eyes on me. "This time I get to be a proper part of it. Where you go, I go. Anxious too. He'll protect us, won't you?"

Anxious yipped from my arms, so I let him down and he circled us, eyes casting around for deadly archers, then sat and kept watch. I pulled off his earmuffs so he looked more menacing, and he shook himself out, most likely feeling odd now he could hear properly.

Most people were either up at the beer tent, gossiping and watching from a distance, or had retreated to their tents and campervans, but a surprising number were still milling about in front of the stage, hoping to catch a glimpse of the ageing ska star who'd truly given them a night to remember. The lights were up, putting everyone in stark relief, until they dimmed and people begrudgingly headed for the safety of the beer tent.

We nipped around the side but were stopped by security. After a word, they let us through because Moose had already informed them we'd most likely be coming, and walked backstage then stopped. Onstage, police, security, and the band were in groups talking loudly with little in the way of order.

DS Kate Moss stood as we approached and shouted, "Will everyone be quiet!? I can't hear myself think. Officer, please escort the band from the stage."

They protested, but the officer insisted, so they were shown the way out. As they passed us, we told them how sorry we were, but none of them said anything; the shock was just too much. They left, numb, like zombies.

"What are you doing here?" said DS Moss with a glower as she spied us.

"We thought we might be able to help," I said.

"Because that's what Max does," snapped Min, coming to my defence.

"Oh, well, excuse me," said DS Moss, dripping sarcasm. "I'll just step back and let Max here solve this for me, then. Well, who did it, Max? Who's the maniac that goes around shooting ageing ska singers live on stage?"

Ignoring her, I took several steps forward and stared down at poor Pete. "Goodbye, Major Two-Tone. At least you went out doing what you love." I don't know why I did it, and I'd suspected him of murder, but I saluted.

His eyes were open, staring lifelessly at the rigging. Pete's arms were still spread wide, the stain on his chest dark now as the blood began to dry in the intense heat. The arrow looked like a prop, a dark shaft with no branding, the flights orange plastic. Strangest of all was the peaceful look on Pete's face and the broad grin he still wore. I think he truly would have enjoyed the infamy this would cause, and no doubt it would make sales of their clothes and music skyrocket.

Thoughts whirred in my head, too fast for me to keep up with, and something began to tug at my subconscious. What had we already seen that told us who did this? Could it be as obvious as it being the guys from Ernie's band? Both Doc Crocs and Sizzlin' Stu loved archery and had been teaching adults and older children every day in the top field well away from the rest of the festival-goers.

What about the people manning the circus? They had a number of skills and had run short courses for the younger ones to learn archery along with more traditional circus activities.

Could it have been Ernie himself? No, I knew he would never stoop so low. Who then? Thoughts buzzed past and I watched them, but nothing stopped to present itself. Just endless images of people we'd met, the bands we'd seen, the lighting and sound engineers, the food vendors, the stallholders, security and police. It could have been any of them.

"Solved it yet?" snapped DS Moss.

"No, but I will," I grunted as I turned to confront her.

"You... What did you just say? How dare you!" DS Moss' face turned puce as spittle flew and she jabbed a finger into my chest in a very unprofessional manner.

"I said I will," I said louder, standing my ground. "You dismissed everyone's concerns about Dutch's death being murder, and just because you don't like it here and dislike the people. We told you it was murder, that it was obvious, but you said you knew better. Don't for one minute tell me this isn't related to his death. Someone is taking out headline acts on the main stage, and now there's no denying a murder has taken place."

"They weren't headliners," sneered DS Moss. "There was another band on after them. Well, that won't be happening now. I'll have this dump shut down."

"Good luck trying," I snapped. "If you shut it down everyone will leave, then you'll never find who did it. What will you tell your boss, eh? That you messed up twice? And as for the band tonight, I don't think you have any choice but to let them play?"

"Oh, and why is that?"

"Because I can hear them already. I'm guessing they're on the other stage. Try stopping that now. But if I were you, I'd get people over there pretty quick in case anyone else is murdered."

DS Moss cupped an ear, then glowered at me before barking orders to the officers and talking hurriedly into her phone, calling for assistance.

"Nobody touch the body!" she ordered, before rushing off the stage, leaving us with the officers, Moose, another security guard, and a stunned sound engineer.

"Can I get on and sort out the wires?" he asked an officer.

"Um, I guess," the officer shrugged, most likely more used to explaining where the toilets were than dealing with murders at festivals.

"Bit of a wild one this year, eh?" said the engineer with a wink. We stared at him, dumbfounded, but he just grinned, then rolled up a cable.

"Do you get things like this happening often?" asked the other security guard.

"Mate, this is the music business. We get all sorts. Murder not so much, but nothing surprises me these days." He traced a wire back to a junction box then disconnected it and began winding it up, like this was a regular occurrence.

"What do we do now?" asked Min.

"I think we better leave the officers to deal with this and check everyone's okay," I said.

"You don't think the killer will go after Ernie and the others, do you?" she asked, eyes never still as she scanned for danger.

"It's doubtful, but I'd still like to know where they are. Whoever is doing this either hates ska or has a motive that puts everyone at risk."

"Like?" Min's eyes roamed as she moved closer to me. Anxious pushed against my leg, insistent, so I picked him up and he snuggled down, glancing at poor Pete.

Paramedics arrived as we left with Moose, but they were too late and I assumed Pete wouldn't remain where he was for long. People were milling around, and from the chatter it was obvious most believed this was pretend. A finale for a rocking show as tightly choreographed as the whole act had been.

Maybe that was for the best. At least they weren't panicking. What they were doing was buying an incredible number of T-shirts. The queue was massive, and getting longer by the minute, even with the main act now kicking up a storm on the other stage. How were they allowed to play? Why were they so sure they wouldn't be next? Did they even know?

"What is happening?" I sighed, my fingers catching in my knotted hair after so much dancing and ensuing chaos.

"I wish I knew. Max, this is getting out of hand. Who uses a bow and arrow?"

"Someone very confident of their own abilities, and with a serious grudge," was all I could imagine. "Look, there's an engineer. Let's ask him how the other band are playing."

I hurried over to the harried looking man and asked, "Did you set up for the other band? How come they're playing?"

"Someone said there was an issue on the main stage so they just jumped right on up. We had no choice but to get them sorted. Bit nuts if you ask me, but they reckoned it was Major Two-Tone pulling a fast one."

"A fast one?"

"Yeah, causing drama so he wasn't upstaged by that guy dying yesterday. Most people reckon it's a ruse. He's not really dead, is he?" The engineer brushed thick dark curls from his face, the strobing lighting from the other stage making him look almost skeletal with deep shadows under his eyes.

"He's dead. Someone shot him with an arrow."

He chuckled, eyes twinkling with mirth, then his smile faded and he frowned. "You're serious?"

"Deadly."

"Blimey. Hasn't anyone told the band?"

"They must have. Surely? They think it was just part of the show?"

"That's what everyone reckoned. Maybe I should go talk to the guys and get them to turn everything off. What do you think?"

"It's not up to me. What did Benny Nails say?"

"That the show must go on. I just saw him arguing with that detective. Right moody mare isn't she? Anyway, stuff to do." He wandered off, whistling.

"Why are they not bothered by this?" asked Min.

"I get the feeling they think we're in on the prank and it really was Pete doing a grand finale for the show. If it was, it worked, because they're selling tons of stock. If he wasn't dead, he'd be rubbing his hands together."

"But he is dead, and this wasn't part of the show, so what should we do?"

"We need to find Benny Nails, and we need to find Ernie and the guys. Where are the other members of Pete's band?"

"Not far away at all." Min pointed and we both stared, agape, as we studied the remaining members selling T-shirts, hoodies, and hats. Laughing with customers, shaking their heads, taking money, and processing credit cards.

"I think we need to have a word with them first," I grumbled, then we stormed over, wondering how on earth they could be so callous.

I spied the leatherworker who'd hidden Pete's knife, so politely interrupted his conversation with another man and asked if we could have a word. Understandably confused, he nevertheless agreed, so I got straight to the point and asked, "Why did you take a knife from Pete? We saw him hand it to you, then you took it into your bus."

"What business is it of yours?" he grumbled, fiddling with his incredibly long dreadlocks.

"Dutch was stabbed yesterday, and now Pete's dead. Isn't that reason enough?"

"The guitarist was stabbed?" he asked, frowning.

"Yes, and now there's been another murder," said Min, glancing at me, confused.

"Blimey, I thought it was an accident. And look, Pete isn't dead. That was the show, right?"

"No, it was real," I said. "So, why did you take the knife off Pete?"

"Look, you got it wrong. I don't like your tone either, mate. I lent the knife to Pete. He wanted to cut a guy rope or something. I bumped into him and he'd forgotten all about it, then got worried he'd get into trouble for carrying it around. What's it to you? You aren't saying I had anything to do with this, are you?" he asked, stepping close to me, his breath sour.

"No need to get angry. We just wanted to know. Thanks for clearing it up. Sorry if I caused offence."

"You're alright, mate," he laughed, face softening. "Poor Pete. We go way back. I always bump into him on the festival circuit. I can't believe someone finally put the grumpy old sod out of his misery." With a nod, he left, leaving Min and I standing there, unsure what to make of his attitude.

"That was..."

"Weird?" suggested Min.

"Yes, very, but I think he was being truthful."

"Come on, we need to have a word with Pete's 'friends' and ask why they don't seem concerned he's dead." Min scowled as we watched them happily selling records and stickers as though this was the happiest day of their lives.

Chapter 11

"What are you guys doing?" I demanded after we hustled our way behind the stall, Moose suddenly appearing and making a broad path before us.

"Cleaning up, mate," said the drummer.

"Making a killing." The sax player grinned wickedly.

"Some help here," shouted a woman in band merchandise who was in charge of their stall.

"You can't be serious?" said Min. "Your friend, your bandmate, is dead, and you're selling T-shirts?"

"It's what Major Two-Tone would have wanted," said the sax player with a sneer and a haughty huff. "Don't you go judging us."

"He died literally a few minutes ago," I said. "Aren't you worried the killer will get you?"

"Killer?" he asked with a frown. "What are you on about?"

Min and I exchanged a glance, utterly bewildered and with no clue what was going on.

"He got shot with an arrow. He's dead," I explained slowly.

"Yeah, we know. But it was an accident, obviously. Nobody's going to do it on purpose. We were going to go have a beer to calm down after what happened, then Shaz here called us over as everyone wants a T-shirt. What can you do?"

"Guys, I mean it," hollered Shaz. "Come help."

With a shrug, they both went to serve the eager customers, giving them the banter about this being the last time they'd ever be able to buy them. People laughed and joked, clearly believing this was a stunt, but eager to part with their money nevertheless.

Moose raised an eyebrow at us and asked, "What should we do?"

"Leave them to sell their gear, I guess," I said, not knowing what else to say.

We backed away, squeezed through the throng, then bumped into DS Moss with a team of people.

"You again," she hissed.

"What's happening?" I asked. "Everyone seems to think it's pretend. They're buying all the clothes and the other band is playing. The engineer said someone told him to let it go ahead as there was just a fault on the main stage. You aren't going to stop it?"

"I tried," she shouted, actually stamping her foot. "Nobody will listen to me, and I spoke to Benny Nails but he refused to pull the plug. Unless my boss makes some calls, I can't shut it down. But I think it's for the best anyway. It's better if people don't panic. How we're going to find the murderer is what I'm more concerned about. It could be anyone. This place is ridiculous. Look at them. Why are they buying those stupid T-shirts?"

We turned and watched the grinning people clutching their purchases tightly, then I gasped as a woman pulled her T-shirt on over her vest and spun to show her boyfriend, beaming with delight.

"Wait! Look," I said.

"At what?" asked the DS.

"That can't be a coincidence, surely?" asked Min as our eyes met.

"What are you two fools talking about?" she snapped, glancing at the people hanging back beside her, clearly impatient.

"The design on the shirt. Look at it."

"No way," gasped Moose as he lumbered forward and grabbed the man who had slipped his T-shirt on too. He spoke softly to him and the man slapped him on the back, then paraded around in front of us, clearly a little worse for wear.

"Stand still, you stupid man," ordered the DS.

We studied the black T-shirt, then Moose turned the guy around and he swayed back over to his girlfriend before they headed for the bar.

"They're all the same. A black silhouette of Major Two-Tone, and the band name, set against a bloody red background," I noted.

"With an arrow sticking out of his chest," added Min. "The red is for blood. The arrow is exactly what happened to him. How is this possible?"

"This is becoming ridiculous." DS Kate Moss spoke to the officers waiting for her instructions, then they stormed over to the stall and hauled the protesting band members away before marching them towards the security cabin.

"They must know something. I'll speak to them later. Now, if you don't mind, I need to escort the team to the murder scene." With a curt nod, she led the way, everyone scurrying after her like scared rabbits.

Moose scratched his head, then asked, "This was planned, wasn't it? It had to be. Think they were all in on this? A dramatic finale gone wrong? A way to sell their clothes and get some infamy?"

"It's beginning to look like that," I said. "Or someone saw the shirts and decided to copy the image. That's an option."

"And much more likely. We need to talk to the band properly. Maybe that's why they are acting so relaxed and happy. Maybe this was a setup and they thought Pete was alive."

"You don't think he could be, do you?" I asked, glancing back to the stage access.

"I think we need to go back and check. Maybe this is a twisted joke."

He was dead. Still very dead. The arrow was real, the blood was real, the press of police, paramedics, and other officials was real. Major Two-Tone was no more.

We left once again, now sure that something was going on that we couldn't understand but would reveal itself in due course.

Anxious was fast asleep in my arms, exhausted by the late night and the commotion. We moved to the back of the large crowd watching the headline act, and they were kicking up a real storm. People danced, sang, and were having a thoroughly good time, oblivious to what had really happened.

Moose spied Benny Nails so we hurried after him as he headed to the beer tent, but Moose whispered that we should hold back for a while just to see. We agreed, so watched Benny talking happily to people who stopped him for a chat, the ageing hippy relaxed and with a ready smile for those he knew or knew of him.

When there was a gap in the crowds, we hurried forward and I called out. Benny stopped and turned, all smiles, but his smile faltered for a moment when he spied us, then he was all friendly again.

"Are you enjoying the show?" he asked, glancing at each of us in turn.

"Benny, what is happening around here?" I asked.

"How'd you mean?" He scratched at his belly, his face red from either drink or something else.

"I mean Pete just got shot, the headliners were told to play, and everyone's carrying on as normal. The Third Skatallion were selling merchandise and the T-shirts have got Major Two-Tone with an arrow sticking out of his chest. What gives?"

Benny leaned in close so we huddled together. "I think we need to go and have a chat. Follow me." Benny led us around the side of the rammed beer tent into a small and very scruffy cabin, clearly a temporary breakroom for the bar staff. Half-eaten sandwiches, scores of discarded paper plates, and numerous empty plastic pint cups littered the corner next to a microwave. The sink was obsessively clean, so clearly someone was trying to do what they could, but failing to keep up with the influx of new rubbish.

Benny scowled at the state of the harshly lit room, then sank into a brown chair and indicated for us to sit. We perched on the edge of the sofa and another chair, none of us liking the look of the stains.

"Benny, you know me," said Moose. "I've worked here for years. Something isn't right. I don't just mean the murders, I mean everything. Why aren't you doing something? Why is everything carrying on? I understand it's best if this is kept quiet, but it seems like you've turned Pete's death into a stunt that nobody believes is real."

Min and I stared at Moose, slack-jawed, as he wasn't normally a big talker.

"That's the most I've ever heard you say," chuckled Benny as he dragged his fingers down his cheeks, leaving white trails over the rosy glow.

"Come on, Benny, out with it. We said we'd help solve this, and now Pete's dead and everyone's acting beyond weird. What gives?" I stroked Anxious as he whimpered, but he remained asleep, mewling as he felt my touch.

"This is between us, okay?" asked Benny as he glanced at the closed door.

We agreed, but noted that if it was anything illegal we wouldn't sit on it.

"It's nothing illegal, just complicated. Look, I know Pete's dead, and that's awful, but I had to keep everything going. The last thing we need is people panicking. It would be carnage. Dangerous. I figured it was best to make up an excuse so the headline act would play, and it worked. What else was I meant to do?"

"That makes sense," said Min, smiling warmly at Benny who seemed to relax.

"Plus, I'd paid them," he laughed. "But seriously, everyone does think it was part of the show. And with those T-shirts, it stands to reason it was just pretend. I still can't believe how many they are shifting though. It's almost like they planned it."

"Meaning, it was one of the band?" I asked. "They decided to play on it and sell more stuff?"

"Don't be daft! They're good guys, and they were on stage, remember? Look, let me be honest. Pete was incensed when he saw the final product. They all were. I get great deals for it, so some bands prefer to go through me to get their things printed. Not just for the festival, but all year round. It's my other business. It makes sense. I order in huge numbers so get the best rates."

"So what was the issue?" I asked.

"Theirs were a little off. I know it looks like an arrow through Pete's chest, but it's meant to be his, what do you call it? His baton. You know, the short cane he waves about, pretending to be a major in the army. The design looked fine, but when we got the final order it just looked like he had this weird thing sticking out of him."

"They're called swagger sticks. It's a sign of authority. Pete had their logo on the silver end cap. He thought it made him look more important," said Moose.

"So you don't think it's a copycat or something?" I asked Benny.

"No, of course not! Just a crappy T-shirt," he laughed nervously.

"Benny, it looks like an arrow. Either someone decided to make it a reality, or it's one helluva coincidence."

"I just don't know! I'm not sure what to think. I'm stressed, tipsy, and so tired. This is a tough event to organise, and I've been working hard for months trying to get everything perfect. This bother with Pete and the boys was the last thing I needed, but what could I do? They were printed. Nobody seems to mind anyway. It added to the drama of the design, and now... Well, they're obviously going to sell out if they haven't already."

"And all the band members have been taken in for questioning now as the detective saw the shirts too," said Min.

"They'll be released soon enough. I spoke to the lads after it happened, and they didn't seem that bothered. The reality is, the band was splitting up after today. Pete didn't know, but they'd had enough of him. None of them can stand him. Could stand him."

"So this was their last ever gig?" I asked.

"Yep, but they hadn't told Pete."

"Did they hate him enough to get him killed? Cash in on things this one last time?" asked Moose.

"They've grown tired of his sneaky tactics to get gigs and the way he acted. But let's get real. Nobody kills over selling a few T-shirts. They don't make that much money from it."

"No, but what about increased music sales? Now Pete's dead, they might take off in a big way. It happens all the time," I said.

"True. But they would have had to hire a killer. Is that what you're saying?"

"Maybe. Or maybe it was someone close to the band," I wondered.

"But why kill poor Dutch?" asked Moose.

"Good question," sighed Benny. "I'm out of my depth here. Please figure this out. We have the last day tomorrow, and if I'm lucky enough to be able to stay open, I want everyone to be safe."

"Benny, you need to close the place down," I said. "It's absolutely not safe."

"I will not! This is the anniversary and people are here for a good time. Nobody's attacking the punters, and I will not ruin everyone's weekend."

"You have to, Benny," whispered Min to calm him down.

"What, now I have to take orders from the three Ms?"

"Huh?"

"Max, Min, and Moose. You hadn't realised?"

"It's just our names," I shrugged.

"Yes, the three Ms. Good name for a band, although I'd spell it EMS. EMS 3 maybe. Quite catchy." Benny got a faraway look in his eyes, then sighed as he heaved to his feet. "I'm truly sorry for what is happening, and you can't begin to know how much it pains me. This is my darling. All I have. I put my heart and soul into the festival every single year, and now someone is trying to spoil it. I won't let them. If the killer is going to strike again, then you can bet it will be for the headline act tomorrow. It's the old rockers, and they get the biggest crowd. It's why half the people are here. So, please solve this, and solve it quickly. I don't trust that detective, but I do trust you. Do you trust me? I need to hear you say it. This has been the longest day of my life."

"We trust you," I said.

Min and Moose agreed they did too.

"I appreciate your support. Why is there glitter everywhere? I keep finding it wherever I go," he grumbled as he ran his hand over the back of the sofa. "It's those circus people. They fling it about for the kids, but it's impossible to clean up." With a scowl at the state of the room, Benny nodded and left.

"Poor guy doesn't know what to do," said Moose, shaking his head.

"He's utterly stressed and way out of his depth," agreed Min. "But he should shut everything down. What if more people are killed? The bands need to know the risks they're taking."

"That isn't our place though," said Moose. "It's down to Benny and the police to make that call. But I do know that our team will do whatever we can to keep everyone protected. Problem is, there are only a few of us and this is becoming impossible to control. Anyone could be the killer."

"I agree Benny should close the festival, but not that anyone could be responsible," I said. "It has to be someone with a very clear motive that we either already know, or will find out tomorrow. We have to figure this out before it's too late. You heard Benny. If this goes ahead, then it's going to be the last band tomorrow. I think Dutch's death was little more than a way to cause chaos and get Uncle Ernie and his band out of the way for some reason. Make them distracted. Or maybe this is all about the merchandise."

"But for what reason?" asked Min.

"That's what we're going to find out. We need to talk to everyone who has a permanent stall, and we need to talk to Pete's bandmates. I don't even know all their names as we never spoke much. Pete always took the lead and the others left him to it. Tomorrow that will have to change."

"I'll ask around too," said Moose. "I'm on from early tomorrow, but off mid-afternoon. I think I'll keep my security gear on, though, and help out with an extra pair of eyes. Benny's a good guy, and if he's going to keep it open, I'll do what I can."

"You're a good friend to him," I said. "We'll see you around tomorrow, okay? But for now, I think it's time to call it a night. I'm absolutely exhausted."

"Me too," said Min, stifling a yawn. "We'll get together tomorrow and see what we've discovered. Gosh, this is very intense." Min's eyes danced with wild energy and I knew the look well enough by now. It was the thrill of being involved in something deadly serious yet intriguing and mysterious at the same time. I hated to admit it, but I felt the same and it was obvious we had become hyped by this terrible series of crimes.

Moose left, so Min and I weaved our way back to the campsite. I wanted to speak to Ernie but he was nowhere to be seen and didn't answer his phone. He wasn't at their van, either, nor were the others, but I assumed they were simply still at the festival. It felt very strange, and wrong, but there had been no love lost between the bands, and they were still mourning the loss of Dutch, so were most likely drowning their sorrows.

Min and I sank into our chairs and spoke late into the night as people revelled around us. Surprisingly, I think we enjoyed ourselves as much as anyone as we sat, drinking wine, and talking about all manner of things. I felt more of a connection to her than ever, and wished the night would never end.

Eventually, Min staggered off to bed, exhausted, but I remained in my chair, watching the fire dwindle and wondering what tomorrow would bring.

Chapter 12

Min was snoring soundly at seven, in a cute, ladylike way of course, so I left her sleeping. I'd been unable to settle, still buzzing after the madness of yesterday, with endless thoughts whirling around in my head. The worst possible time to dwell on matters is at night. Things go around and around in an endless loop and there's no clarity, but a new day always brings a new dawn, and with it the opportunity to uncover the truth.

A sense of urgency gnawed at me, and I couldn't shake it. Although it wasn't my place to figure this out, I felt a deep sense of loyalty to Benny Nails, even if he was being very obtuse about not closing the festival. Uncle Ernie was family, and I worried for his safety, too, and wanted to find who killed Dutch, a kind-hearted young man with his whole future ahead of him.

Pete, aka Major Two-Tone, may not have been the greatest guy in the world, but even he deserved justice.

The entire thing left me with an uneasy feeling in my stomach. Knives and arrows, T-shirts, and seemingly no concern from Pete's band members regarding his death. It was very unsettling. Shouldn't they care? They'd been together for decades.

What about the DS? Why was she so dismissive of the whole thing? I understood that she wasn't a fan of festivals, but surely her job was important to her? What would she be doing to uncover the truth? How do you go about finding a killer among thousands of people?

You stick to the obvious, that's what. I had to speak to Pete's "friends" this morning, get to the bottom of the whole merchandise thing, and I had to talk to Uncle Ernie and the other members of The Skankin' Skeletons.

After that, there were a few others to question, then I was out of ideas. What puzzled me the most was the seemingly utter lack of consistency and the risky way people had been killed. Knives concealed on someone in the crowd to murder Dutch. An arrow being shot from a secret location to kill Pete. How risky was that? And what if they'd missed? Maybe they knew they wouldn't? Were they that good a shot?

Laughing at myself for letting my thoughts get manic again, I shook it out, grabbed Anxious' flinger plus a handful of poo bags—he'd had lots to eat yesterday thanks to the kind festival folk who couldn't resist giving a cute dog a treat—and we headed up to the dog field.

There are only two kinds of people up and about at seven in the morning at a festival. Those who haven't been to bed yet, and those with dogs. Oh, plus the smug ones who want to get to the toilets and showers first!

We weaved between tents and motorhomes, tiny campervans and massive bell tents, the sounds of snoring all that could be heard. Anxious sniffed around still-smoking barbecues, checking for scraps, then raced off ahead into the field where we spent a lovely half hour with him running back and forth like a thing possessed, never tiring of this simple game. How beautiful a thing it was, and it never failed to put life into perspective. He adored the repetition, the certainty that he knew what was coming next. The joy of simply being alive and using his muscles to play a game that held no meaning beyond it being fun. Wasn't that enough? Maybe it was.

Once Anxious was suitably tired and panting happily, we walked to Uncle Ernie's pitch at a leisurely pace. I was beyond relieved to find him outside with the guys, if looking rather rough around the edges.

"You're all alright?" I asked, hugging my startled uncle.

"Hey, what's with the man hug?" laughed Uncle Ernie, pulling back a little and frowning as he looked into my eyes.

For a moment, I saw indecision, and possibly guilt, but then he smiled warmly and relaxed.

"I couldn't find you last night, and you weren't answering your phone. What happened? Pete got killed and you were nowhere to be found. Any of you." I glanced at the others in various stages of readying for the day, all bedraggled and rather red-faced.

"Yeah, sorry about that. We went to drown our sorrows about Pete's lot putting on such a good show, and got carried away. I tried to call you once we heard what happened, but I was out of charge."

"You couldn't have used another phone?" I asked, watching him closely. I absolutely did not want to suspect my own uncle, but he was acting strangely. They all were.

Ernie mumbled something, his head down, then he removed his trilby and ran a hand through his short hair.

"Sorry, what?" I snapped, exasperated. "Ernie, you aren't making this easy for me. What's going on?"

"We got cornered by that damn detective, that's what!" he grumbled. "They had us in that stupid cabin for ages asking us questions. They suspected me. Me! And the lads. It was ridiculous. After all we went through with poor Dutch, and then she had us sitting there for hours, utterly stressing us out. Reckoned we must have been in on it. Just because some of the lads like to do archery, she reckoned it was enough to get us taken to the police station. Freaked us right out. Then she said you were looking into it as well, so I knew you were okay."

"But you were released eventually?"

"Yeah, but only because Stu threatened her by saying he wanted a lawyer. We all did. She stormed off in a huff and said we could go. I do not like that woman."

"Me either," said Stu as he came over, a wan smile on his face, his grey stubble making him look old and tired, not a funky member of a rocking ska punk band.

"You and Doc Crocs have been teaching people archery, haven't you?" I asked, trying not to sound accusatory.

Stu bristled. "What if we have? We do it every year. Benny Nails pays us extra, and we like to get the chance to practice."

"I'm just trying to figure out why you were questioned. Did you check your equipment?"

"That's the first thing she wanted to do. We brought them down here and went over everything. We know exactly how many bows and arrows we have, and they're still in the van. I don't think we'll be doing any today. It's got me right stressed out this has."

"I bet. Look, I'm sorry you went through that, but at least the detective is trying to figure this out."

"By accusing us," sighed Stu. "We'd never do anything like that. Pete was a right nutjob, and not a nice fella, but we aren't going to murder him. Especially because it means he's got exactly what he always wanted."

"What's that?"

"He's gonna be bleedin' famous, isn't he?" interrupted Doc Crocs. The others grumbled their agreement, and Ernie nodded.

"I guess. They were certainly selling a lot of stock after it happened. Nobody thought it was real. Did you hear?"

They hadn't, so I explained about the sales the band were getting and the mix-up over the logo, and it certainly didn't improve anyone's mood.

The rest wandered off to get ready for the day, banging about in the van and getting short-tempered with each other, so Ernie and I sat in the camping chairs and Anxious jumped up into his lap.

"He always knows exactly what to do," sighed Ernie as he smiled at Anxious, who wagged happily then rubbed against my uncle's hand as he stroked him gently.

"He's a smart boy. Ernie, the merchandise situation seems very peculiar."

"How'd you mean?"

I shrugged. "It feels off. Benny getting the logo design wrong, Pete's lot getting that prime spot for their gear, you not getting a permanent table when you were the headline. It seems weird."

"Max, you're reading too much into it. Benny has to try to accommodate everyone. He has to think ahead. He wanted Pete back next year so gave them the best position, but we got headline status and had to take a backseat for sales. I told you, it's how these things work. Same every year. It's politics, and this is a cutthroat business. We all want to earn a living from what we love, but you have to play the game."

"I suppose you're right."

"So what's the issue?"

"The whole thing reeks. I'm not sure why. Everyone's given a reasonable explanation for how it works, but I suppose seeing Pete's band happily selling T-shirts while he lay dead was a shock."

"It's because they hated him."

"Could one have put a contract out on him?" I asked. "Sorry, that sounds dumb. I'm getting carried away. Who does that?"

Ernie laughed, then said, "I think you need to cool it, Max. You're becoming obsessive. You know it isn't good for you. Take a step back, think things through properly, go over what you already know, but don't focus too much on one thing."

"That's sound advice. Thanks. You know I get way too involved."

"Once you get hold of something, you refuse to let go. It's why you were an excellent chef, but also why you were a terrible type of person to get involved in the business. You're happier now, right?"

"Ernie, like you wouldn't believe. I love this life. The freedom, the chance to relax, be out in nature, take things slowly. But I have this calling. I'm meant to help people, and solve these terrible crimes. I feel like it's my duty to stop bad things happening. I know I get obsessive, but with the mysteries I've taken a more relaxed approach. Just gone through everything methodically and asked questions until I figure things out."

"Then do exactly that, Nephew. Don't fixate on the merchandise, but follow where it all leads. Get justice for Dutch, and I guess for Pete, but for everyone else too. This could be the end of Lydstock otherwise. I'm amazed the press aren't all over this already."

"Most people thought it was a gimmick. I imagine hardly anyone knows the truth."

"Word must have got out by now. And what about poor Dutch?"

"People definitely think that was an accident. And I'm sorry to say it, but he didn't have the same notoriety as Major Two-Tone. It's not newsworthy like he'll be."

"Then you need to get your skates on and solve this. If anyone else is murdered, they'll definitely close the festival early and it might never re-open."

"I'll do my best." With a nod to Uncle Ernie, I called Anxious. He gave Ernie a final lick on the face, then hopped down and trotted after me as we headed up the hill to the main arena.

I had a few things I wanted to check over early this morning, knowing that soon the crowds would start to wake up and I'd lose the chance to snoop in private.

As we neared the entrance to the actual festival grounds, it was clear that things were not as they once were. There was already a large police presence, with a group hanging around outside the security cabin, drinking tea and no doubt grumbling about the early start.

It seemed that the private security company had been asked to beef up its presence, too, as I easily spied double the usual contingent, and no doubt there were plenty more already on patrol and checking for signs of trouble.

After showing my wristband — Anxious didn't have to buy one, which was just as well as he'd spent all his pocket money on Pokemon cards — we were allowed into the main arena. The stages were deserted, the clothing stands empty and closed, along with the other gazebos and food outlets. Only one place was open, serving coffee and breakfast rolls, so I decided to get a drink and risk a breakfast.

After a short wait, I came away with a steaming coffee, a soft roll containing a fried egg, a sausage, two rashers of bacon, and a hash brown all covered in brown sauce as that's what you have at breakfast time when in the festival spirit, which I was trying my best to hold on to.

It was... better than Min's by a little, worse than I'd hoped by a lot, but I ate half, gave Anxious the rest, who wasn't bothered in the slightest by the fatty food, and wolfed the lot before I had the chance to remind him that he needed to watch his weight.

Sipping my coffee, I approached the stage then stopped at the closed engineers' booth and shifted around until I stood where I had the night before. Closing my eyes, I pictured in my mind where I'd seen the arrow, and the angle that it hit Pete. He was slightly to the left of centre stage as I looked at it, meaning the shot must have been fired from behind me to the right.

The arrow was arcing down when I'd seen it glint under the stage lights, the black shaft shiny and deadly fast. So that would mean it had definitely been fired from rather high. I spun slowly, Anxious copying me, and we both locked our eyes on the roof of the cabin we'd spoken to

Benny Nails in. That was a perfect spot. High, but not too high, a clear line of sight to the stage, a solid metal roof, with a sign fixed to the front above the door affording good cover for the killer. If I wanted to get away with murder using such a ridiculous weapon, at such a ridiculous time, with so many people in attendance, then I supposed that was about as good a spot as it got.

Nobody would see you, you could rest on the sign for stability, then once you'd fired it would be easy to duck down, and get off at the rear where it was dark without being seen.

We made our way over, Anxious on full guard duty as he scanned for murderous hippies in tie-dye and oversized fluffy hats wielding large bows, but we saw none. The door was locked, which I was surprised at as what was there inside worth stealing? I put my face to the window and cupped my hands either side, careful not to touch the grubby glass, and peered inside.

The place was just as messy, but someone was asleep on the sofa, tucked up in a brown sleeping bag. There was a hole in the bottom where a foot stuck out, a bright orange sock the only part of the person visible. The sleeping bag had a hood and it was pulled over their face, so there was no way of knowing who it was or even if it was a man or a woman, although, judging by the size of the foot and the shape of the body, I'd put my money on it being quite a large man.

A loud bang followed by muffled cursing startled us, and Anxious darted under the beer tent canopy into the large marquee, still in stealth mode so not barking, which made me proud. I checked if anyone was watching then slid under, feeling guilty and as though I was committing a crime rather than trying to solve one.

Anxious was sitting in front of the bar, hackles raised, head cocked to the side, so I hurried over and squatted, stroking his back as I congratulated him on being so quiet. His head tilted the other way as another bang and more cursing came from the other side of the doorway behind the bar that led into what I assumed was the storage area for the barrels and whatnot.

We crept forward slowly, about as ninja-like as we could be, then I stood and risked a peek; there was nothing to be seen. Suddenly, a shape darted past the open door, making us both jump, and Anxious barked from his position on the bar.

"Who's there?" called a timid voice from the rear room.

"I heard a noise, so thought I should come and check on things. Is everything alright back there? Who are you?"

"I'm the barman. What business is it of yours? Get lost. We don't open for hours. If you want a drink you'll have to wait. I'm setting up."

"Sorry to bother you. Just trying to be a good citizen," I called out, craning to get a look at the man yet to show himself.

"Fine, it's fine. Thanks for checking." Another bang, more cursing under his breath, but it was clear this was nothing to worry about so I helped Anxious down and we left.

It was only once we were outside the beer tent that a familiar feeling washed over me, intense and impossible to ignore.

I dashed back in with Anxious at my heels, then vaulted the bar and raced into the back room, almost sending a tower of empty beer barrels crashing to the ground before I grabbed them.

"Where's the man, Anxious?" I asked as I searched but came up with nothing.

Anxious skipped over to the back door and I flung it open, surprised it hadn't been locked, and caught a glimpse of a man wearing all black rushing away. He glanced over his shoulder as he turned the corner, then was gone. With a black baseball cap pulled low, I didn't get to see his face, just a bushy beard, which really didn't narrow it down much. Half the men here had beards, and the other half were trying to grow one.

Was he security, or did he just dress in black? Was he really working at the bar, or was he a thief?

The murderer? And who was in the staff cabin?

Chapter 13

The cabin door was open; there was no sign of the sleeping man. I hurried inside with Anxious taking the lead, nose to the sticky floor. With so much mess, it was impossible to tell if whoever had slept inside had taken anything, or possibly even eaten here.

The sofa was empty bar a few threads of long hair on the arm, which may or may not have been the man's. Anxious soon got bored and trotted over to the door, but I called him back and patted the sofa. He hopped up amidst a cloud of dust and noxious smells, but took a good sniff around.

"Think you can find him, boy?" I asked. "There's a biscuit in it for you if you do."

At the word biscuit, his eyes darted to my pocket. I patted it, and that was all the encouragement he needed. He sniffed and sniffed, then jumped down, ran for the door, and glanced back.

"So, you've got his scent?" I laughed.

Anxious stared at my pocket, tail wagging.

"Find him first," I said, trying to hide my smile as this was a serious business, especially for him as there was food involved.

As my intrepid pooch raced off, I gave chase, heading in the same direction as the man from the beer tent. Anxious may have been small, but he could outrun anyone when treats or rabbits were involved, although he never managed to match them for wiliness and the ability to change direction at speed.

I tore down the hill after him, wondering what on earth I was doing but certain it was important, then followed Anxious to the right and back up a rise that led to a fenced area reserved for the staff and businesses.

Anxious squeezed through a gap in the fence, but I couldn't go after him. I followed him with my eyes, but he suddenly stopped, clearly confused. I spied a man carrying a bundle ducking behind a truck and then something caught my eye and I noted a slim man in black for a flash before he, too, was gone.

Then I saw another man, and a woman, then a couple, and realised everyone was getting up and the place was full of people. Some wore black, security teams were patrolling, and it was obvious that it could have been any or none of them.

Anxious returned to the fence, came through, then sat, tail wagging, hope in his eyes, but his head was down as he knew he hadn't quite pulled off the chase.

"You deserve your biscuit anyway," I said.

Anxious took it gently like he always did, then searched around for a suitable place to settle. Deciding it was unfair to make him wait, I simply sat on the grass and patted the ground. He flopped down, panting and happy, and tucked in.

The world was waking around us, and I knew I'd never find the two men now. With doors banging open and shut, the familiar sound of zips opening and people panicking as they rushed for hedges or toilets after holding it in for hours, our suspects were gone.

Once Anxious had finished, we weaved our way up to the beer tent then around the side of the cabin. At the back, I found several old beer barrels up against the wall, so told Anxious to keep a look out and bark if anyone came, then clambered up and realised I could haul myself onto the roof by resting my foot on the windowsill.

As I rolled over then sat up on the already hot metal, I was shocked to find two pairs of eyes staring down at me. One was a definite glare, the other a friendly twinkle.

"DS Moss, and Moose?" I blurted, feeling almost out of my own body as it was so surreal. "What are you doing here?"

"I might ask you the same question," snapped DS Moss. "And him." She jabbed a finger at Moose, who smiled happily and shrugged.

Standing, I studied the pair and how they acted for a moment, sure there was something going on between them. DS Moss looked almost guilty, and was dishevelled, when normally she didn't have a hair out of place. Moose wore his usual black security gear but was looking way too keen, and his eyes kept flashing to the DS. Did he like her? Seriously?

"Did you come up here together?" I asked. "Do you have a, er, um... thing going on?"

"Thing?" asked the DS.

"You know, a secret arrangement to meet and, um, get to know each other?" I asked in as polite a way as I could muster.

"A secret affair, you mean?" asked Moose, grinning from ear to ear.

"Yes, I guess," I shrugged, way out of my depth.

"Absolutely not!" barked the DS. "I came to investigate, as that's what we detectives do, even though I know you don't believe that. And then Moose arrived just after me. Now you're here too. What are you both up to?" she asked, peering at me like I was the guilty party.

"I'm not up to anything. It was bugging me about how the shot was fired, so I traced it back to here. It's the perfect vantage point."

"And you could hide behind the sign," added Moose.

"Exactly!" I agreed.

DS Kate Moss sighed, shook out her mess of red curls, causing Moose to sigh, then admitted, "I had the exact same thoughts. Maybe you two aren't as incompetent as I'd suspected. But you are interfering in an active investigation. You've contaminated the scene and neither of you are wearing gloves."

"I have mine in my pocket," I said. "I would have put them on if I touched anything."

"And I've got mine too," said Moose happily. "We aren't dumb."

"No, seemingly not. Now, what else has been happening?" she asked, glaring at me.

For a moment, I contemplated not telling her, but that was churlish, so I explained about the people in the cabin and beer tent, what I saw, even what Ernie had said, and the strange merchandise situation. She listened without interrupting, just like Moose, and when I finished she was quiet for so long I thought she was too angry to speak.

"Max, I owe you an apology. You're good at this, and I mean it. As skilled as any detective, and better than some I know."

"Wow, thank you."

"But this is still my investigation, and what I say goes. Maybe it is good you're involved, and you certainly seem to have the right questions to ask and an uncanny knack for being in the right place at the right time, but watch your back."

"Yes, I will. Sure. Moose, what about you? Anything of interest?"

Moose scratched at his stubble, lowered his eyes, and admitted, "I got nothing. I asked around, spoke to quite a few people, checked with the team, and nobody saw anything suspicious. Everyone's being super-vigilant, but there's no sign of who did this and no real leads apart from here."

"Then we need to find the people who were here," said DS Moss.

"Didn't you look in the window, DS Moss?" asked Moose.

"Please, I think both of you can now call me Kate. And no, I didn't. Only Max did. I tried the handle and it was locked, so came straight around the back then up here. We all obviously just missed each other. I must have come when you and Anxious chased after the suspects, Max, then Moose turned up."

"So what's next?" I asked.

"What's next is we find who did this. I'm going to make a report to my boss, who isn't happy about any of this, especially the festival remaining open, but Benny is adamant, and to be quite frank I think our best chance of finding the killer is to ensure everyone stays here. But it's not without risk."

"And can't people come and go as they please anyway?" I asked. "You see cars driving in and out all the time."

"Exactly. We're taking the details of anyone who leaves early, but it's probably fruitless. I get strong hunches, and my hunch is that whoever is doing this isn't finished yet. They won't leave. Not yet."

"I agree," I said.

"They're going to wait until this evening and do something utterly epic," said Moose with too much gusto.

"Then find this murderer," said Kate with a nod to us both.

We took turns getting down, then stood around rather awkwardly. Anxious got the attention he craved from Moose, then turned to Kate and cocked his head, as if sizing her up. It was as though he knew the dynamic had changed and he was deciding her fate.

Seemingly satisfied, he stood, wagged happily, and walked over to her. She squatted, glanced from me to Anxious, then stroked his back gently.

"It's stiff but soft at the same time," she laughed. "Thank you for letting me stroke you, Anxious."

My best buddy yipped, then sauntered off, sniffing around to impress Kate.

"He likes you. That's a good sign."

"It is?" asked Kate, standing, then brushing down her smart and utterly out of place dark suit.

"Yes. It means you're a good person. Anxious always knows. He's very smart."

"And so is his owner." Kate actually blushed a little, then nodded to us and marched down the path, back to being a no-nonsense DS.

"Did you really not find anything out?" I asked Moose.

"Not really. I spoke to all the staff last night, apart from one, and nobody had anything to say. They didn't see the killer, obviously, and there was no sign of the bow or any arrows. Everyone was shocked, and our boss is livid. He told us to check anyone suspicious, and to ensure we are careful, but this has shaken everyone. We're meant to protect people, ensure the rules are followed, and report anything suspicious, but so far nothing."

"Who didn't you speak to?"

"One of the guys. He wasn't on duty yesterday evening. It wasn't his shift, and I couldn't find him. We have our own camping area where the bands and businesses stay, but he wasn't there either."

"That's where the two men I spotted went. The one from the bar and the other from the staff cabin. Think he might have been one of them?"

"He is a big drinker," admitted Moose. "He could have been sleeping it off in the cabin, or he could have been pilfering beer."

"Is he the kind of person to do that?"

"Max, we're security, not police. We come from very mixed backgrounds. Some are ex-soldiers, others are ex-cons. Plenty of us used to just be regular people, or bouncers, or normal guys like me who enjoy the work."

"What appeals so much?"

"I enjoy the travel, being out and about at cool places like this, and you get to meet great people. Most of the time, the job consists of wandering around looking menacing and checking bags for contraband at the entrance. Basic stuff. It's a very rewarding job because I basically get paid to have a walk and stay mobile. And before you say it, yes, I know I'm overweight, but I like my size. It's who I am."

"I wasn't going to say anything about your weight, and I certainly don't think you're just a regular guy, Moose. You're a dark horse, aren't you?"

"I told you, I'm a normal bloke who's a bit of a ninja too."

"You sure are. Now, can you get me into the private camping area so we can have a word with this missing guy? Surely he's there by now? Especially if he was one of the men I saw. What's his name? What does he look like?"

"Jordan Flanagan. He's a wiry bloke, about your height, long dark hair, streaks of grey, with one of those faces."

"One of those faces?"

"Yeah, you know. Looks like he's had a hard life. Done things. Been through tough times but come out the other side. He likes a drink and is a bit of a chancer. Not anything illegal, but he's different than the others. Doesn't mix much, keeps to himself, not too friendly, but good at his job. His shift will be starting soon, so he should be at his tent or getting breakfast. Let's go have a look."

Moose led the way, with Anxious trotting happily alongside him. There was definitely something about this man. He was undeniably big, but his movements belied the bulk. Moose should lumber, but he glided like a true wild animal. Not threatening, just the opposite. Discreet, confident, but not swaggering. Like he belonged. In fact, it was as though he could vanish with a click of his fingers if he so wished.

As I thought this, he did disappear. I stopped, looking around as Anxious pined, and sniffed the ground, then sat, head cocked, as perplexed as me.

"Over here, guys," called Moose, waving from the fence.

"How did you do that?" I panted as I hurried over.

Anxious raced ahead, wagging, enjoying this new game of hide and seek.

"I told you, I watch a lot of Youtube videos and read a lot of books," he beamed. "Come on. Let's go talk to Jordan."

Moose followed the fence line until we came to the entrance. He chatted with the two men on duty then we went through; the gate was shut firmly behind us. They were taking no chances, and it was obvious everyone was jittery and no doubt under strict instructions to keep the area for staff and bands under tight lockdown.

We weaved through the sea of tents and vans large and small, ancient and modern. I watched my steps carefully, mindful of the guy ropes, but Moose never once looked down, and never came close to tripping. Moose stopped at a small blue tent facing away from everyone else. A man was sitting in a camping chair with his back to us, leaning forward as he tended a small, disposable barbecue at his feet.

As a group, we eased around until we were in front of him and he jumped, dropped his tongs, and hurriedly tried to hide a can of beer behind his back.

"It's just me, Moose. No need to hide the beer."

"Blimey, Moose, you scared me half to death. What are you doing sneaking up on a guy in the morning before he's even had his brekkie?"

"Just checking on things. Jordan, this is Max. Max, this is Jordan." Anxious barked, so Moose laughed and said, "And this is Anxious."

"He doesn't look anxious," said Jordan with a frown before he pulled out his beer and took a sip, daring us with his eyes to say anything about him drinking before he started work.

"It's his name, not his emotional state," I explained, wishing yet again we'd come up with a different name, but knowing in my heart I wouldn't have it any other way.

"Whatever." Jordan waved it away as of no concern to him, then retrieved his tongs and turned his sausages on the smoky barbecue.

"You know what happened last night?" asked Moose, jovial and relaxed.

"Sure. Dude got shot with an arrow." Jordan shrugged, eyes on the beer and sausages.

"I tried to find you, but couldn't. Everyone else was helping out."

"My shift was over. I went for a few beers. No crime in that. Look, Moose, and Max, what are you doing here? What do you want? Why is this guy even here?" He glanced at me, red-rimmed eyes making it clear what kind of night he'd had.

"We're helping look into it," I said. "Trying to figure out why anyone would do it. Any insights? Did you hear anything?" I noted the brown sleeping bag sticking out of his tent, then my eyes trailed down to his feet. I spied orange just visible above his boots. Unless orange socks were somehow all the rage, this was the man who'd been in the bar staff's cabin not long ago.

"What are you gawping at?" hissed Jordan, staring at his boots. "Got a thing for feet, do you?"

"No. Do you?" I countered, the words sounding ridiculous because they were. I needed more sleep; my mind was not as sharp as it should be.

"What's with this guy?" Jordan asked Moose. "What business is this of yours?"

"My uncle is the singer with The Skankin' Skeletons and their guitarist was killed. Now Pete. I'm trying to figure it out. Any insights you might have would be appreciated. We don't want to intrude."

"You are intruding, and like I said, I went for a few beers. That's not a crime now, is it?"

"Of course not," soothed Moose. "Hey, where did you sleep it off last night? Hear anything? See anything?"

"Dunno. Just woke up in a daze this morning then wandered back here. It was a bit of a session, if I'm honest. Enjoyed the buzz and the band. We done?"

"Sure, Jordan, we're done," said Moose with a relaxed smile. "Take it easy, yeah?"

"Sure, Moose, you too." Jordan's eyes locked on mine —there was no friendliness there—then downed his beer and turned his sausages.

At the gate, Moose promised to catch up with us later, so we left him to his shift. He was on patrol duty so we'd undoubtedly bump into him.

"What do you think, Anxious? Could it have been Jordan? He was evasive, not very friendly, and he was definitely the one in the cabin, right?"

Anxious barked his agreement, but just because he'd slept where we assumed the arrow had been fired from didn't make him a killer.

It certainly made him a suspect though. What could the motive have been? I had plenty to think about.

Chapter 14

Anxious and I were about to return to see if Min was awake when we spied her coming through the security checkpoint. She waved, looking like an angel in her short denim cut-offs, an arresting green vest that showed off her trim figure, and, of course, her hat. I couldn't help smiling as she skipped up the path. A pang of guilt and utter bewilderment took hold of me for a moment, the pain visceral. How had I let this beautiful, kind, caring, compassionate woman ever get away from me? How did I deserve her? Did I? I forced it down, I had to, because I knew I could never be good enough for her but would spend my life trying to be.

"We were just coming to get you," I said, taking hold of her hands and bending my knees as she reached on tiptoe and we kissed.

"No need!" she beamed. "What an amazing day. It's gorgeous already."

"Sure is. The temperature will be through the roof by lunchtime."

"Then we need to make the most of the morning, and have a nice lunch before we come up to watch the bands. There's all sorts going on today, and it's going to be awesome!"

"What's got into you today? You're very chipper," I laughed.

"Chipper? Have you ever said that before in your life?" Min teased.

"I don't know, but it suits your mood. Sorry we weren't there when you woke up. Did you miss us terribly?" I winked, and Min giggled.

Anxious whined, so Min fussed over him as she said, "I did, actually. It's been lovely waking up with you both just there. Especially this little guy."

"I know I shouldn't be jealous of him, but I am," I admitted with a smile, even though it was true.

"So, what's been happening? What have you uncovered? Fill me in on everything."

We got a coffee while I explained, which didn't take too long, then Min asked the inevitable question. "What now?"

"Now I want to speak with the circus people. They have bows and arrows for the children, see lots of people, and get around the whole site. If anyone knows anything, I'm sure it's them. They mix with everyone up here, but go around the camping fields, too, and you know what kids are like. They talk. Maybe one of the youngsters said something that might be of help. Have you spoken to any of the performers?"

"A few. I bumped into the clown just now and he was quite chatty. I think he fancies me, actually, but you can't take it seriously when a bloke in oversized shoes and a red nose is asking for your number."

"You didn't give it to him, did you?" I asked in a panic.

"Max, relax. We went over this. I wouldn't ever do that to you."

"Good. And especially no clowns," I teased.

Min laughed again, revealing her throat as she flung her head back. She really was in an incredibly good mood.

"Slept well, did you?" I asked, intrigued by her high spirits.

"I did! I had the best night's sleep ever. Vee is so comfortable. But it isn't just that. It feels safe in the camper. Cocooned, and like nothing can harm me. I thought I'd find it claustrophobic, but it's the opposite. It is cramped, and it's hard to move about when the bed's down, but when it's folded away I adore it. I even sat in there to have my coffee earlier, wondering where you guys were."

"Sorry about that. We were up early and didn't want to disturb you. Plus, I wanted to check out the cabin. Good job I did."

"It sure was. Now, let's go molest clowns." Min beamed at her own joke.

Things were beginning to liven up around the site now most people had surfaced, craving sustenance or entertainment. The food stalls were opening, performers were limbering up, some acts were already at it. A magician with a top hat and wand was entertaining children, the fire-eater was having her breakfast of flame on a stick, much to the delight of both young and old, and as we approached, it was clear that the circus had been busy for a while.

Hula hoops, ribbons on sticks, unicycles, and all manner of odd equipment lay scattered around outside the big top, while inside children were practising their skills, walking beams or ropes, being taught how to juggle, or dressing up in costumes.

"Fancy a go on the tightrope?" asked Min with a wink.

"Crocs aren't good for that. But you go ahead.

"Maybe I will." Min tugged at her lip, but stayed put.

"Changed your mind already?"

"I'm not sure flip-flops are the best either."

We were saved by a man about our age with a mop of wild hair dyed in multiple colours with a friendly smile and a clear eye for Min.

"The clown, I assume?" I asked as I put out my hand.

"It's the nose, right? It's a dead giveaway." He honked his nose by pinching with his fingers and clearly squeezing a horn behind his back, but smiled warmly, so we shook.

"We've already met, but didn't get introduced. I'm Max. I think you already know Min. And you are?"

"They call me Bonbon, but the name's Brian," he said with a shrug.

"Nice to meet you, Bonbon," I said.

"And nice to meet you again," said Min, stifling a laugh. "Sorry, I'm just in one of those moods today. Isn't it a beautiful day to be alive?" She skipped around us, then stopped, shook Bonbon's hand vigorously, then beamed as she leaned forward and peered at him. "You look so different without your clown make-up and clothes on. You don't really have big feet at all, do you?" she teased.

"Um, no, they're just pretend," he stammered, looking from Min to me.

"You have pretend feet?" asked Min, suddenly serious.

"No, the shoes."

"But they were real. I saw them."

"I mean, they're oversized shoes, but my feet aren't really that big. Look, are you alright? You're buzzing for so early in the day. Been at the beer already?"

"No, of course not! I'm just happy. The sun's shining, it's going to be a great day full of fun and music, and we're alive! Isn't that something to celebrate?"

"It sure is," said Brian.

"Min, are you sure you're okay? I'm happy you're happy, you know that, but you're overly excited and I'm not sure why." I tried to catch her eye as she looked everywhere but at us.

"I'm fine. Just slept well, and after the horrid things yesterday, it brought it home how lucky I am. How lucky we all are. Bonbon, were you chatting me up earlier?" Min peered at him, eyes snapping to attention, but smiling rather coquettishly.

"Um, well, you know." Bonbon scratched at his head, glitter falling, as he glanced at me. "Are you two together?"

"Yes, and no. It's complicated," I admitted.

"We are," said Min, then slapped her hand over her mouth.

"We are?" I asked, trying to hide my stupid grin.

"Kind of. We were, and now we're..."

"Yes, friends," I said to help her out. "Bonbon, can we ask you a few questions?"

"Sure, what's up? This isn't about me talking to Min, is it? I didn't mean to step on your toes, mate. I mean, she's a lovely lady, but I'd never try to muscle in on anyone who's already taken."

"No, not that. I assume you heard about the killing last night? Maybe you saw it? And about the night before?"

"I heard about the guitarist dying, but that was an accident as far as I know. And last night was a stunt, right? Major Two-Tone isn't really dead, is he? I thought it was part of the show. We were around, watching bits of it, but the youngsters are allowed to be up so late that they pester us to do tricks and things like that. What's this really about?"

"They weren't accidents or part of a show. It's real. Surely you must know that?"

"We don't get told anything. Benny's a good guy, but he doesn't keep us in the loop. Why isn't the place closed if there's a murderer?"

"So nobody will freak out, and so everyone can have a good time. Did you see anything last night?"

"No, nothing. Just the bands and the kids and way too many hula hoops. I was up the top doing tricks, riding a unicycle, but it got a bit much. I got changed and cleaned myself up, then ducked into the beer tent for a break. Then the kids don't recognise me. They only remember the clown."

"I bet. What about the other members of the circus? Can we have a word?"

"Sure. I'll go round them up. It'll have to be one at a time so we can entertain our fans, but it shouldn't be a problem. I can't believe Pete's dead. I've done this gig for years and he's always here. It won't be the same without him. Poor guy. I assumed they were just doing a grand finale. It was certainly impressive." Bonbon smiled weakly, then ruffled his hair. Glitter rained down again onto his shoulders like happy rain.

"You're very sparkly," laughed Min to lighten the mood.

"Yeah, the stuff hangs around for weeks. We go through a load of it with the youngsters. They do little shows in the big top and we throw it around. They love it. I need to wear a hat. I find it everywhere." Brian bent and ran both hands through his hair. This time it was even worse, with the red glitter blowing on the soft breeze. Anxious barked excitedly then ran through it, getting covered, but then he paused, looked at Brian, and cocked his head.

"Hey there, little fella. You like glitter, do you?" asked Brian as he squatted beside the curious dog.

Anxious yipped, tail wagging, but when Brian reached out to stroke him he backed away.

"Anxious, what's wrong?" I asked.

"There's nothing to be afraid of," said Brian with a look to us. The bracelets on his arm jangled and Anxious barked then moved to my side.

"Maybe he doesn't like the jewellery?" I offered.

"Maybe," said Brian as he straightened. "I'll go have a word with the others and you can speak to them. But I don't know what they can tell you."

Children ran around, full of energy and joyous at the freedom the festival afforded, while parents sat happily on the bank, watching, or taking the opportunity to catch up on missed sleep. The other members of the troupe were either demonstrating how to use equipment or showing the children the dressing up area, so Brian did the rounds and pointed at us. It was obvious some weren't too happy about what he said, which was strange, but all ended the conversation with a nod.

"Why are they so unhappy about talking to us?" wondered Min.

"I'm guessing that they get a lot of grief. Fairground and circus folk still have a bad reputation with some people. Especially fairground workers."

"That's not still a thing, surely? Everyone loves the circus and the fair."

"Not as much as you. I'm amazed you haven't dressed as a clown or done the high wire yet."

"I do fancy having a go." Min stared wistfully into the big top where the high wire was, not that it was exactly a large circus or the wire very high, but I still didn't fancy her chances but remained quiet.

Brian returned with a young woman and we asked her a few questions, but she clearly didn't know anything. Next was a seasoned veteran of the circus, but he wasn't very friendly and had little to say apart from that we shouldn't go judging them because they lived an alternative lifestyle. We promised we weren't, and when I mentioned that I lived in my campervan he mellowed somewhat, but still had no insights.

The other woman was more affable. Min got on well with her instantly because she was the high wire performer and Min asked about it, but like Brian she'd thought it was a stunt the band had pulled so couldn't help us.

Last, but by no means least, we spoke to the owner of the circus.

"Hi, you're the owner?" I asked.

"I am. Look, I don't know what you said to everyone, but they aren't happy. Why can't people leave us in peace?" asked Mal.

"We honestly didn't mean to give the impression we were accusing anyone of anything. We thought that as you're active all over the site you might have heard something," said Min.

"It's true then? Pete's dead? That's a real shame. Nobody tells us anything. Benny should know better. We should have been warned. If acts are getting killed, we have a right to know."

"So you haven't spoken to the detectives or any officers?" I asked.

"No. But we get up early and the young 'uns are already here waiting to be entertained, so we're in our own little world down here. Ah, here they come now," grunted Mal as he looked past us.

We turned to find DS Moss and an officer approaching, so I asked hurriedly, "Mal, have you heard anyone say anything that you think might help us figure this out? Any issues with the bands that you're aware of?"

"Just grumbles about the stalls, but that's the same every year. Everyone wants the best spot. And, of course, there's always bad feeling about who gets to headline, and who gets to play when. The usual nonsense. We stay out of it and keep our heads down, but I haven't spoken to anyone since last night apart from my team. We work long hours and stick to our own company mostly, but let's get real here. If I had spoken to the killer, they aren't exactly going to admit it, are they?"

"No, they aren't. Thanks for your time."

Mal grunted, then hurried away before Kate and the officer arrived.

"We meet again," said Kate with a frown.

"Yes, and I'm guessing you had the same idea as us?" I asked.

"Like I said, you are definitely good at this," said Kate, although she didn't look too happy at being beaten to talking to the people here.

"Thank you. We didn't mean to interfere," said Min. "We just thought we'd see if anyone had heard anything, but they didn't even know Pete was dead. Like everyone else, they thought it was an act."

"I'll talk to them anyway. But word's getting around now, and by lunchtime I imagine everyone will know what happened. I can't say people are exactly panicking, which is concerning, but this is becoming a desperate situation."

"How so?" asked Min.

Kate moved in close, checked we weren't being overheard, especially by the children who were beginning to take an interest in the police officer, and said, "Because there's a killer on the loose. The entire festival should be shut down, but Benny refuses and I can't get it done myself. The acts are being informed, which is why I'm here, and they need to decide for themselves whether to stay or leave. A few bands have given us trouble when we suggested they leave, but so far nobody has. They want to stay. This festival means so much to everyone, but, frankly, I'm amazed. Now, I have a busy morning, so if you'll excuse me?" With a curt nod, Kate and the officer approached the big top where Mal and the others were grouped together. Brian caught my eye and nodded, then turned back to the others as Kate called to them.

"That was all very..." gasped Min, shaking her head.

"Weird?" I suggested, feeling perplexed by the way the circus staff acted and how Kate was.

"Definitely. Let's go and get another coffee and think this through."

The festival was truly waking up now. People were everywhere, and from the overheard snatches of conversation, it seemed everyone was excited by last night's craziness and actually looking forward to the day ahead.

We queued for coffee then grabbed one of the small, two-seater picnic tables and sat opposite each other, neither of us speaking as we watched people coming and going with breakfast rolls. Others were setting up for the day with camping chairs or blankets, coolboxes, and even cushions and umbrellas.

The heat was building along with something else. It took me a while to figure it out, but then I realised what was different about today.

"Can you feel it?" I asked Min once I understood what was happening.

"I can, and it makes me worried."

"Think this is what it's all been about?"

"What do you mean?"

"It's an air of excitement, right?"

"Yes, exactly. You can feel it all around. Everyone's intrigued by the murder. They're waiting for something else to happen."

"So maybe this is what the killer wanted. A build-up to tonight. They're ensuring that there will be a record crowd this evening, and people have all day to talk about it and spread the word until the main acts go on. It'll be utter madness."

"You know who we need to speak to, don't you?" asked Min with a dangerous glint in her eyes.

"Oh no, I don't think that's a good idea," I warned.

"Max, of course it is," she said with a smile and a dreamy look.

Chapter 15

"I just adore Danger to Life," sighed Min.

"You're pulling that weird face again," I teased, smiling as Min began to lose the plot like she always did when she thought about them.

"I am not! I just appreciate their music."

"Min, you are a grown woman, but whenever you think about the band you revert to being a teenager and fawning. I am not going to take you to talk to them. You'll forget your own name, start drooling, and won't be able to think straight."

"That's very insulting. Like you said, I'm a grown woman. I won't lose my self-control because I'm talking to a bunch of ageing rockers."

"You don't fool me for a moment. You're already getting flushed and doing that weird smile like you're standing in front of Simon Le Bon. Remember what happened when you met him?"

"That was an accident! You promised never to bring that up again," growled Min, casting her laser eyes my way.

I ducked, managing to escape the brunt of it, but I still checked my hair for singeing. "Phew, that was close," I grinned.

"Max, stop being mean!" Min pouted, but smiled too.

"See, now you're all gooey-eyed because you're thinking about Simon Le Bon, aren't you?"

"Maybe. But nothing like that will happen again."

"Min, you bumped into him while he was at a festival with his wife and you literally dropped to your knee."

"Slipped."

"Then you bowed your head."

"Had something in my eye."

"And when I helped you up, you grabbed hold of the shirt of Duran Duran's singer and asked him to marry you!"

"I did not. I asked if he'd say hello to me, not marry me!"

"That's not exactly true, now is it?" I giggled.

"No, not exactly," whispered Min. "But I was younger then, and I adore Duran Duran so much. When I saw him, I suppose it's possible I got a teensy bit excited. Only a little."

"And asked him to marry you even though you were married to me then, and his wife was with him."

"But he didn't say no, did he?" asked Min brightly.

"True, he didn't. But I don't think you meeting Danger to Life is a smart idea, do you? What if you do something like that again?"

"I won't. I'm grown up now."

"You were grown up then. It was only four years ago. And I know how much you love these guys, even if they are a bit dated now."

"Dated? Dated! Are you nuts? They're the best rock band in the whole world."

"And have been for about forty years. I like them, too, but I'm not star-struck. Maybe sit this one out?"

Min pouted, then brightened and said, "You won't be able to see them anyway. They'll be in a big, fancy tour bus well away from everyone else and there's no chance of just walking up to them and having a chat."

"I don't think you have any idea about their status now, do you? Danger to Life were a huge band playing all the big stadiums back in the day, but that was a long time ago. Now they do the festival circuit, and if they're playing small places like this, they aren't going to be staying in the lap of luxury. I saw their van up where the other acts are, and they have tents the same as the rest of us."

"Tents? Are you sure? I assumed they'd have a huge tour bus with bedrooms and a fancy bathroom and a nice place to chill out. They can't be in tents."

"They are. Okay, let's make a deal. If I can get us in there, do you think you can hold it together? Min, I know you idolise them, but we need to ask them serious questions. They might be responsible for this."

"Don't be daft," she laughed, then punched me on the arm, a little too hard.

"Ow! What was that for?"

"It was only a gentle tap."

"I see that look in your eyes. You're already excited, aren't you?"

"Maybe a smidge. You can't tell me that you aren't."

"I absolutely am not. They're just musicians. There's nothing special about them. Apart from being great at what they do, obviously."

"I bet you'll be a right wobbly mess and won't be able to string two words together."

"Won't happen," I said, grinning as Min began rubbing her hands together. "Let's go and find Moose. He'll be able to get us inside the compound. I don't think the guys on the gate will let us in without him, even though I was up there earlier to speak with that security guy."

"Great idea! But we don't really think Danger to Life had anything to do with this, do we?"

"That's what we're about to find out."

Min skipped along beside me, and her good mood was infectious, so soon Anxious was running laps around us, tail like a windmill in a storm, with no idea what we were up to but happy regardless. As we hunted for Moose, it dawned on me why she was so exhilarated this morning.

I stopped, turned to her, and accused, "You're so upbeat because you knew we would have to speak to the band, aren't you?"

"Maybe I did realise this morning that this led back to them, and that I might get to speak to the man himself. Oh, he's so handsome."

"I knew it! That's why you've got your extra short shorts on and that tight top and why your hair looks so lovely. And you smell amazing."

"Don't you dare sniff me," warned Min. "And I didn't make any extra effort at all. I always try to look nice. You know that."

"You are such a bad liar."

Min grabbed my hand and dragged me up to the various craft stalls as we spied Moose, trying, and failing, to hide her eagerness.

"Oh, isn't Ivan the best? He's got such an amazing voice. If anything, it's got better over the years."

"I think you might be right. It's what you'd call gravelly. Like he's chewing on a mouthful of rocks when he sings."

"And he looks more handsome than ever. He's always so tanned, and with that long hair of his and... and..."

"Calm down. You're hyperventilating. He's a rock legend, that's for sure, but with that huge hoop earring and the way he always has his shirt unbuttoned, he looks more like a pirate than anything."

"I know! Isn't it awesome!?"

"Min, you're wearing out the exclamation mark," I teased, happy to be here to witness her joy. She deserved this, and so much more, but if meeting her favourite singer could make this weekend memorable for the right reasons, then I was happy to at least try to oblige.

"Moose. Moose." Min waved as he turned, so she dragged me over with Anxious darting off ahead to get a fuss from his new friend.

"Hi. What are you looking so excited about? Has something happened? Min, why are you smiling so much? Pleased to see me?"

"We figured we should go and speak to Danger to Life and see what they think about all this, but Min's got a major crush on Ivan, the singer, so is acting like a schoolgirl."

"It's not a crush. It's respect for a great singer and a great band."

"I can tell you're lying," teased Moose. "You want access to the band enclosure?"

"Yes please," I said. "Have you met them?"

"Sure. I've met most of the acts. I spoke to Ivan earlier, actually, and the other guys. Just to explain about what happened and ensure they still want to play. The detective lady was up there, too, telling everyone about it, but so far everyone's really relaxed and want to stay. It's a bit weird, isn't it?"

"That's what we said, but then we understood that the bands will get record numbers of people watching, which is good for their future. Everyone's excited rather than worried."

"But they should be worried," said Min. "So we need to speak to Danger to Life and explain. What if Ivan's the real target?"

"Or he's orchestrated everything so they get all the attention tonight," mused Moose. "Maybe it's a way to be the main focus and drum up more interest for their appearance?"

"I had the same thought, but Min won't hear a bad word said about Ivan and the others. Which is why I said it would be best if she hung back and let me speak to them."

"Don't be daft, you two. Ivan would never do anything like that. He's a legend." Min skipped off, then turned her head and shouted, "Hurry up."

Moose and I shrugged then followed after her.

After getting us through the now very tight security, he led us to the area reserved for the bands who decided to stay at the festival either out of necessity because of travel arrangements, or because they got a free pass so decided to enjoy the event. Most seemed to have come for the entire three days, and I recognised several faces. Of course, at least half the bands decided to camp in the regular fields, mixing with fans and enjoying the atmosphere, but those who either didn't want the attention or preferred to stay where the facilities were better and there were real toilets, took advantage of the chance to relax somewhere more private.

"What's he like?" asked Min as she looped her arm through Moose's, much to his surprise.

"Just a guy with very shiny long hair and a jaw that's too square. Seemed nice enough."

"What did he say? Tell me," insisted Min, dragging Moose to a stop.

"Nothing much. Just that he was sorry about Pete and Dutch, but he wouldn't be scared off by someone trying to ruin things. I promised we'd have as much security as possible, and there will be police, too, but I warned him that it might not be enough. He and the others all said the same thing. They owed it to Benny Nails and everyone who had paid to put on the best show of their lives."

"Those were his exact words?"

"Um, yeah," shrugged Moose.

"Did you hear that, Max?" squealed Min. "The best show of their lives!"

"I heard," I laughed, shaking my head.

"Wow, you really have a thing for Ivan, don't you?" Moose glanced at me and asked, "You aren't jealous?"

"Oh, I'm jealous alright, especially because Ivan is such a hunk." I winked at Moose, but Min was oblivious.

"Isn't he divine?" she sighed.

"They're just up here." Moose strode off, but Min shouted, "Wait! I'm not ready. So sudden? How's my hair? Should I keep the hat? Do I look a terrible mess? Is my lipstick on right?"

"Min, you look lovely, smell even better, and I don't think you need to worry. Come on." I took her hand and we followed Moose and Anxious, who had both got bored and somehow vanished.

We walked past a large motorhome then Min gasped and stopped dead in her tracks.

"Um, you might want to loosen your grip a little," I whispered as her eyes locked on a group of people.

Anxious was in Ivan's lap having a tummy rub while Moose was chatting happily with the men.

"What? Eh? Whose hand?"

"Mine. Loosen your grip. It's just a man, not a god."

"He looks like a god."

"Min, he's in his sixties and sitting in a camping chair rubbing Anxious' tummy."

"I know. Isn't it amazing? I'm never letting Anxious wash again. He's been blessed with Ivan's hands."

She relaxed her grip, so I shook my hand free then approached with Min so close I almost fell over, but righted and slowed so she didn't make this even more awkward than it was already becoming.

"Ah, here they are," said Moose loudly. "Guys, I was just telling everyone that you wanted to have a word. They don't mind."

"Of course not," came the deep, raw voice of Ivan. "Max, I hear you're quite the amateur detective. That's some fine work you've done lately. You should be proud."

"Thanks. That's kind of you to say."

The other band members agreed that it was good work I'd done, and that they'd heard about some of the cases I'd helped solve, but then they excused themselves, clearly used to Ivan taking the lead when talking to fans or others and most likely not wanting to get too deeply into any of this. I didn't blame them.

I stepped between the chairs, nodding to the men as they left, then took Ivan's proffered hand and we shook. "I think Anxious likes you," I noted, as the little guy squirmed under his strong hand, enjoying the attention from his favourite rock star.

"He's a friendly guy," laughed Ivan. "I love dogs, and have three that we rescued, but they're at home. They don't like touring too much and prefer to hang out on the sofa. Now, Moose here tells me you have a few questions. Sorry the guys vanished, but they've been talking to security and police all morning and have had enough. Everyone just wants to get on with having a good time, you know?"

"I understand, and it's not a problem. But you're okay talking to us?"

"Sure. Moose is a great guy and I trust him. If he vouches for you, then I'm good. Um, is this lady with you? Is she alright?"

I turned to see Min rooted to the spot, visibly trembling, eyes as wide as saucers. Her colour was up and she kept tugging her vest with one hand while pulling at her lip with the other.

"She's rather star-struck, I'm afraid. We're both fans and have seen you play a few times, but Min really, and I mean really, thinks you're the greatest."

"Then she's got great taste," laughed Ivan, sounding like he was gargling gravel. "Min, is it?" he asked, his big blue eyes smouldering as he smiled, the laughter lines crinkling. I felt sure he was innocent in all this, but looks could be deceiving, and the reality was that the band would have an incredible amount of attention this evening if they did play.

Min took a stiff step forward, then stopped. Her face went through a series of strange configurations, and I surmised she was trying to smile, but all she managed was a lop-sided smirk, then a frown, then she resorted to pushing her lips up before giving up and exhaling loudly. She dropped to her knees, crawled forward, and lay her head in Ivan's lap beside Anxious, who began licking her nose excitedly. Finally, Min flung her head back, gripped Ivan's knees, and blurted, "Marry me, Ivan. Marry me now!" She gasped, looked around at us, and promptly keeled over backwards, out cold.

"Told you she was a fan," I laughed, before realising this might be serious and kneeling to check on her.

Min's eyes opened and she shot up then asked, "Did I do okay? I didn't make a fool of myself, did I? I can't remember."

"No, you did fine," I said, face straight. "In fact, I'm not even sure if Ivan knows you're a fan at all."

"Oh, gosh, I better tell him. Where is he?" Min followed my gaze, so turned, realised Ivan was right there, gasped, then began crawling forward again.

"Min, I think you need to sit on the blanket and try not to move," I suggested as Ivan carefully put Anxious down then stood to help.

Now towering over Min, she made one last attempt to secure a proposal, and grabbed for Ivan's faded dark jeans but missed and collapsed, much to Anxious' renewed delight. With her face prime for licking, he got straight to work until I called him off and asked him to sit.

"Is there something I should know about?" asked Ivan kindly. "Some medication she needs?"

"No, honestly, she's never normally like this. Min's utterly besotted and doesn't do well when meeting famous people. Maybe just take a seat and I'm sure she'll recover."

"Maybe you're right." Ivan sat back down while Moose and I took a chair once he invited us to sit.

"I'm so sorry," gasped Min as she pulled herself together. "I don't normally get flustered, but I've always wanted to meet you and I think I blacked out. Did I do anything silly?"

"No, nothing at all," said Ivan, keeping his face straight and winking at Min, eliciting a gasp.

"Oh, that's a relief. Sorry to be a simpering fool. You must get it all the time."

"Not as often as you'd think, and certainly not from women as young and pretty as you. Um, no offence. I assume you two are a couple?"

"No, I'm single," blurted Min, then slapped her hand over her mouth. "Sorry, Max, that was awful of me." She turned to Ivan and explained, "We're divorced, but best friends, and just seeing how things go."

"That's beautiful. You two were made for each other, I can tell."

"Thank you," I said, meaning it.

"Guys, I gotta go, but I'll see you later?" asked Moose.

"Sure. We'll catch up this afternoon. Keep your eyes and ears open," I said.

"You too." He nodded, then left to continue his patrol.

"Now, what can I help you both with?" Anxious barked, causing Ivan to chuckle and add, "Sorry. What can I help all three of you with?"

Satisfied, Anxious lay down and curled up beside Min. She patted him, but I don't even think she realised.

"Are you going ahead with playing tonight even though you know the risk involved?" I asked.

"We have to. We can't leave everyone hanging. We've been coming here for years and it's our favourite festival. We know so many people, and wouldn't dream of letting Benny down. He's been good to us, and helped us out when times were tough. Our comeback onto the scene and increased sales is down to him. Benny's a decent guy."

"He is. You're sure this is a good idea? You aren't worried?"

"Worried? Of course I'm worried. If frontmen are getting shot at, then I'm a prime target. How can anyone possibly protect me from that? But don't you worry, we have a few ideas up our sleeves. Old Ivan will be okay."

"Please don't die," gushed Min.

"I'll try not to. And besides, I know who did it, so everything will be sorted out soon enough."

Chapter 16

"Who?" asked Min with an overt gasp, like Ivan had the answers to life, the universe, and everything.

I was intrigued, and waited out his just as dramatic pause as the tension built. Even Anxious scooted closer, ears twitching in anticipation.

"There's more to this place than meets the eye. It's the same at every festival. Lots of backstabbing, plenty of intrigue, and often some mystery too."

"You mean like over the merchandise? You didn't get the best location this year, did you?" I asked.

"Nah, not that." Ivan waved it away as inconsequential. "That's just smart business. Benny knows how much the headline spot means to everyone, so he tries to be as fair as possible. We take a backseat for the physical sales, but get to headline, and we still got a very decent permanent pitch. It's all good. It's not like it's going to make us rich. Most people who come to see us already have plenty of our gear, so we never do gangbusters with our stuff. We do well with vinyl and cassettes as the old stuff is back in fashion now. Shirts and hoodies not so much."

"Then what?" asked Min, acting closer to normal now she'd got over her crush a little.

Ivan leaned forward in his seat, wincing as his back creaked, and whispered, "Booze. It's the booze."

"Sorry, but you've lost me," I admitted.

"It's new people running it this year. Surely you noticed?"

"I didn't think too much of it," I said. "We usually bring our own, and get a few pints, but Min likes Prosecco and I hate crowds. It's always rammed in there. But, yes, new faces behind the bar."

"And they aren't as friendly. Efficient, but not as chatty," said Min, her eyes still locked on Ivan as though he might do something jaw-dropping, like bursting into song.

"Yes, well, it's a long, rather sad story. To make it simple, Benny broke ties with the previous company because last year he caught them watering down the beer and he's adamant they didn't pay him the proper cut of the profits. He was part owner in the business, helped build it up, but when he went over the books he had a massive argument with his partner then sacked him. Got his money back after a lot of legal wrangling, but nothing was proved. Benny got a new business partner and this is the first year. It's not going so well. Different beer and cider, the prices are higher, and from what I hear sales are down."

"Even with this heat? I'd assume they'd sell more than ever."

"So did Benny, but apparently not. From what I've learned over the years, there's nothing like a wet festival for record sales. People take shelter in the beer tent rather than being out watching the bands, so they buy more. When the weather's perfect, everyone's outside and enjoying the music and the performers."

"But how does this mean you know who the killer is?" I asked.

"It's Benny's previous partner. I've seen him hanging around. He looks shifty, always has. Tall, skinny fella with lank hair and a face only a mother could love. I bet you he sabotaged the festival out of revenge. I'm amazed Benny hasn't chucked him out, but he's a real softy and too kind-hearted. Needs to toughen up and stop being such an old hippy all the time. Peace and love is great, but now and then you have to bash heads."

"That's the guy I saw in the beer tent this morning," I said.

"What's this?" asked Ivan.

I told him about the man in the cabin used by the beer tent staff, and that someone had run from the back room, explaining that Moose had led me to the security guard sleeping it off, but we hadn't traced the other man.

"Sounds like him. He's beyond annoyed with not having the contract, and I bet he was trying to tamper with stuff. You should tell Benny. No, actually, I'll call him and explain. Get him to have the lines and barrels checked. Last thing he wants is no beer on the final day. Can you imagine?" Ivan shuddered and Anxious whined.

I turned to my dog, only to find him fawning over Ivan like Min, both of them hanging on his every word. "Since when do you find beer tasty?" I asked Anxious.

He licked his lips and barked.

"Someone's been doing things they shouldn't," laughed Ivan.

"Yes, no more beer for you," I told my dejected dog as he hung his head. "Have people been letting you have a cheeky taste? They should know better."

"But, Ivan, even if the beer tent has been sabotaged, that doesn't mean this disgruntled man would kill people. Are you sure about this?" asked Min, finding her voice at last.

"No," Ivan admitted. "But what else could it be? I bet it's a grudge over beer."

"What's this man's name?" asked Min.

"Crispin Cotteril, but everyone calls him—"

"Don't tell me. It's Crispy, isn't it?" I sighed.

"You got it!" beamed Ivan.

"There's one other possibility, and we haven't looked into it yet. Something Benny Nails said the day Dutch was killed. He said it was probably Campbell, a big festival promoter whose been pestering Benny to sell up the rights so it can be turned into a bigger event. What do you know about him?"

"He's around, keeping an eye on things, but he comes and goes. He isn't staying here. He prefers nice hotels. Not that I blame him for that."

"What's he like?" asked Min.

"Good at what he does. Great, in fact. We play a few of his festivals every year. He pays well, better than Benny, but it's a much bigger operation. Huge events, lots of bands, but we never headline at those places. We're more mid-listers. It is what it is," said Ivan, wistful, and clearly still pining for the glory days.

"Would he stoop to murder?" I asked.

"Would anyone? But no, I don't think so. Sure, he wants to take over this place, but it's small potatoes for a guy like Campbell. Hardly worth his while."

"Ivan, thank you so much for your time. It's been a pleasure to meet you, and we appreciate you talking to us. If you do play tonight, good luck. You always rock. But watch your back and don't take any chances. Stay safe."

Everyone stood, so I shook Ivan's hand, then we turned to Min. She reached out slowly, her hand shaking, and Ivan grasped it, pumped vigorously, then pulled Min in for a hug, winking at me over his shoulder. Min gasped, nearly collapsed, but Ivan lifted her up until her feet were off the ground then settled her gently. He kissed her cheek.

Min blushed, put her fingertips to her face, and sighed.

With a chuckle, I led Min away, nodding to Ivan. Anxious darted back, got a head rub, then caught us up.

We weaved through the mass of tents and vans, got through security, then paused the other side of the fence.

"You okay?" I asked.

"Awesome. Am I dreaming, or did I just get a cuddle and a kiss from the rock god himself? Did Ivan hug me?"

"He sure did," I laughed.

"Um, did I say goodbye? Did I speak? It's all a blur."

"Yes, you were very polite and said a nice goodbye. He smiled and said it was lovely to meet such a pretty lady. You were very calm and told him you loved his music and it was very kind to spare the time for a chat."

"Oh, good, because for a moment there I thought maybe I'd made a fool of myself and gone all gushy. That would be very silly." Min tittered into her hand, coy, then sighed before skipping off with Anxious yipping by her side.

I hung back, leaving her to check what was on offer in the pop-up shops, so I could process things. The list of suspects was growing, but we were barking up the wrong tree. I didn't know how I knew, but I was certain. I would track down the promoter and this "Crispy" bloke, I wouldn't be a very good amateur detective if I didn't, and I supposed I should speak to DS Moss about them, see if she had anything to add, but the reason behind everything was something I already knew.

The other mysteries had been simpler in many regards because they were in small places with much fewer suspects. Here, with thousands of people, so many businesses, old rivalries, backstabbing, arguments over merchandise, beer, festival rights, who would headline, the best pitches for the food stalls, and on and on it went. How on earth was anyone meant to uncover the truth when so many people could have a vendetta against either Benny, another band, a rival stallholder, or just someone who preferred drum 'n' bass to classic rock or punk-infused ska?

What made this more unusual than the other crimes I'd encountered was the way it was done. Stabbings and arrows? It was astonishing. Whoever did this could blend in with a crowd, slip away unnoticed, and nobody was the wiser. Who had that set of abilities?

I chuckled as a picture of Moose popped into my head. The big fella certainly had the skills, appearing from nowhere as he did, then vanishing like a ninja despite his bulk and amiable personality. But Moose? No, that was ridiculous.

Uncle Ernie? Again, no chance. He was family. His band? No, they would never hurt Dutch, and how could they? The other members of The Third Skatallion? Again, they were on stage when Major Two-Tone met his untimely, but admittedly dramatic and impressive demise. Unless one of them had hired a killer, then no, it wasn't them either.

Benny Nails himself? The idea was ludicrous.

Jordan Flanagan, the security guard with a drinking problem? My gut said no, and that he'd just been sleeping off a rough night. The state he was in, how could he have shot an arrow and hit his target when he most likely couldn't even walk straight?

This brought me back to the members of Ernie's band. They did archery, and they'd all disappeared halfway through their rivals' set. But they hadn't killed Dutch.

An accident? Maybe Dutch did just somehow rip his leg on something. Maybe it was one of Ernie's buddies?

Or maybe it was a youngster who'd been messing about with a bow and arrows and it was an accident too?

None of the many possibilities sat right with me, but I was convinced it would slot into place eventually. The problem was, we were running out of time. If I didn't uncover the killer before this evening when Danger to Life —a worryingly apt name—hit the stage, then Ivan had a high chance of never performing again. It would break Min's heart, and leave fans distraught. I liked Ivan—he was surprisingly down to earth for someone who had seen and done so much—so vowed to do what I could to protect him and get justice for everyone else.

Mind a little more clear, I caught up with the others and put the worry aside while I enjoyed their company and we bought a few souvenirs.

Lunchtime was fast approaching by the time we'd finished, with crowds now gathered for the early bands. We caught a few songs, but it wasn't quite our thing, so we headed back down to the campsite and the relative peace and quiet of the field.

Min was still in high spirits, but I knew her well enough to realise she was heading for a crash. She was absentminded and not quite steady on her feet, the excitement of the day too much for her. In fact, I realised that I was the same. I couldn't focus, or even cut the bread properly when I made her favourite lunch of pork in crusty rolls with English mustard. A sprinkle of Maldon sea salt, and it was ready.

"Max, you shouldn't have," Min gushed as I handed her a plate stacked with rolls, then set down a bowl of crisps, some lemonade, and a few things to nibble on. I joined her on the blanket under the shade of the sun shelter and smiled.

"You deserve it. And I'm going to make a lovely early dinner too. We need to relax and enjoy ourselves."

"We do. We've been having a nice time, though, haven't we?" Min placed her lunch down and took my hands in hers. "It's been great, hasn't it?"

"It's been incredible to spend so much time with you. I couldn't have asked for more. I've enjoyed myself a lot, of course. The three of us together makes it perfect."

"I've had the best time too."

"Not just because you met Ivan?"

"Max! No, because we've got on so well. How we used to. It's like years ago when we came here and had one of the best weekends of my life. Perfect. I know it's terrible what's happened, and I feel guilty for being happy, but that's alright, isn't it?"

"Of course it is. We have to enjoy life. That's what it's for. To find the wonder in the everyday, enjoy the company of others, and be happy."

"I'm so glad you said that." Min beamed, a truly deep smile of pure happiness, then brushed at her hair self-consciously. I caught a faint trace of her perfume and shampoo on the gentlest of breezes and I knew that life didn't get any better than this.

Anxious slid between us on his belly, gliding forward, eyes locked on the food, tongue out and tasting the air as he glanced at me then continued like he hadn't been seen. Ninja dog he was not.

"Anxious, why are you the cutest dog in the whole world?" giggled Min before she scooped him up and rolled around.

Anxious forgot about food for a while as they played, then was given a little treat while we settled down to eat.

I needed to do something normal, so insisted that Min take it easy and relax after lunch. She looked exhausted, and I felt the same, so I unfolded the bed for her and she went inside the campervan, turned on the small fan, and lay down.

For a while, I was lost to mundane but enjoyable tasks like washing up, drying the few dishes, tidying the outdoor kitchen, and even prepping for tonight's one-pot wonder. As it was the last night of the festival, I decided to do something different, and hoped Min would enjoy it.

With everything readied, I popped my head inside the camper to find Min propped up on the pillows, eyes half-closed.

"You done?" she asked dreamily.

"All done. Try to sleep. I'll take the chair and have a nap outside."

"No, come and join me. Have a lie down. You need it. Look at you, you poor thing. Anxious is already here, so let's nap together." Min patted the bed and smiled, so I slid my Crocs off and clambered onto the bed then lay beside her with Anxious between us.

It was warm, but not uncomfortably so with the fan on. Just the heat of Min's body and Anxious pressed against us in the small bed. I refused to let myself dwell on the fact that tomorrow she would be gone, and simply let my mind drift into the perfect state between being awake and sleeping where the world dissolves around you and sound is muted as you drift off to another universe.

I slept better than I had in years, and lay there, my eyes closed, when I woke up, the sound of Anxious' snoring and Min's breathing better than any music I would ever hear.

"Are you asleep?" Min asked some time later.

"No. Are you?" I teased.

Min nudged me in the ribs and laughed, so, of course, Anxious took that as a cue for it to mean playtime. The little scamp yawned, then scooted up the bed until his face was between ours and began licking, his tail thumping against the bed.

"Think it's time to get up?" I laughed.

"Someone seems to think so. But I don't want to. Can't we just hide away in here and never go outside again?"

"That would be lovely," I sighed.

Before I knew it, I was startled awake. I checked my watch and found we'd gone back to sleep for another hour. Min opened her eyes and smiled. Anxious was sitting at the foot of the bed, watching us, then bounded over for a cuddle, just as happy as us at this brief moment in time.

Reluctantly, we rose, casting sheepish grins at each other, knowing it was best not to say anything, but both aware this had been a special time. It might not be forever yet, but it was a step in the right direction, and we knew it.

I left Min there while I put the kettle on, the sounds of the campsite and the music drifting from the stages slowly creeping back into my awareness.

The sun was shining, the heat stifling, but I wouldn't have it any other way. It was perfect.

Chapter 17

"I won't be long," called Min as the kettle whistled and I jumped up to turn it off before my brain exploded from my ears.

"No problem. What are you doing?"

"Just putting the Rock n Roll bed away. I think I've got it figured out."

"Need a hand?"

"No, I'm okay." Min grunted, the campervan rocked, then she shouted, "Ow! Ugh, hey, what's this?"

I dashed inside with Anxious beating me to it, to find Min standing in the middle of the admittedly small footprint, the bed half folded away, and staring at a sheet of crinkled A4 lined paper.

"What have you got there?" I asked, stepping closer.

"I'm not sure. I was trying to do the bed, but I think I did it wrong, and this slipped out from under the cushions. It was tucked between the slats. I got my fingers jammed and it pushed through."

"A drawing? A letter?"

Min's eyes scanned the page, then she looked up and said, "I think we better take this outside. You might want to sit down."

"Min, what is it? A note like the other one?"

"Not quite, no. Where is it?"

"Here, in the drawer." I reached over, keen to read this latest find, but first retrieving the small message I'd discovered when fixing a cupboard. A slip of brittle yellow paper with the words HELP ME scrawled in scratchy handwriting.

I backed out with Anxious "helping" and sat in my chair, coffee forgotten. Min emerged, hair mussed, but more beautiful than ever even as she slumped into the chair beside me.

"This is incredible," gasped Min before she handed me the page.

My eyes drifted down to the thick paper in my hand and I read the scrawled message, sure it was the same handwriting. I held the previous note up and checked properly. "They're from the same person. Here, take a look." My heart hammered as I passed it over.

Min studied both messages then nodded. "It looks the same. You're right. Max, what does it mean? I know you dismissed the other note as someone making a bad joke, but this? What should we do?"

"I'm really not sure. Can I take another look? Or maybe read it to me so I can listen?"

"Sure." Min patted my leg, full of sympathy and confusion, then cleared her throat. "Please, please help me. I've been stuck in this van for weeks now, and I don't know if I'll ever get out alive. If you find this, then my name is... That's it, just the squiggle." Min lowered the page and gripped it tight in her lap.

"Min, someone was trapped in Vee. Held prisoner. This must be a joke."

"It has to be. How could you keep someone locked in a campervan? You'd smash the window or shout for help, surely?"

"If you were able to. Maybe they couldn't do any of that. But I don't understand. How could both messages be from the same person? One's on ancient paper hidden behind a panel in the cupboard, the other is modern lined paper under the bed."

"That's easy. The little message is just written on whatever they could find, so looks old. Maybe it was a scrap they discovered. But it's the same handwriting, so it means both are more modern."

"Can we find out when the paper was made?" I wondered.

"Not without a forensics expert. Someone who's a specialist. Who could do that?"

"Nobody I know."

"Do you think it's genuine? Is someone playing a twisted joke?"

"That's what I assumed about the previous message, but now I'm not so sure. This is entirely different, and very serious if it's true. I'm not sure what the goal is by playing a joke like this. Saying someone's kidnapped is a serious business."

"Then we need to discover who wrote it. Contact the previous owner and see what he has to say?"

"The only issue with that is he had Vee for absolutely years and that means he's the one who held this person hostage. If I get in touch, he'll know I'm on to him."

"We don't want to give the game away. But he lived locally?"

"Not too far away. About an hour from here. Maybe it's best to go and visit him rather than phone. I don't know what I'd say anyway. Hello, did you keep someone in the campervan you sold me? Would you mind telling me who it was and what happened?"

"Most likely, they were murdered. Max, we should tell the police. Or will they even believe us?"

"This is evidence, so I suppose they should. They'll investigate, and maybe that's for the best. What do you think?"

Min's eyes were ablaze, and she kept them locked on mine when she said, "We should do it ourselves."

"But the police need to see this. It will have fingerprints on it. They might be able to trace who it was."

"Then ask the DS for a favour. She's much more friendly now, right? Tell her about it and see if she can get the fingerprints run, assuming there are any."

"But then it's an official investigation. Is that for the best?"

"No, just ask for a favour. Don't explain it all."

"It's rather obvious. If I give her the page, she'll see the message. If I don't, we're hindering an investigation into a possible kidnap and murder."

"Then you should give it to her. Have you got her number?"

"Yes. I'll call and we can go hand it in." Concerned, I made the call and Kate agreed to meet me. She said she'd been meaning to get in touch anyway, which was a shock.

Careful of the page, I took a photograph, placed it in a clear sleeve, then left Min and Anxious at the van while I went to find the DS. Things were very busy now, with music echoing around the site, people coming and going, everyone having a great time. Children especially were making the most of it, running around, laughing and screaming, dirty, covered in glitter, and determined to stay up super late tonight. I spied Bonbon with a group of youngsters waving long ribbons around and laughing as they got themselves tangled.

DS Moss was at the security cabin with a few officers, several private security staff, and a group of very serious-looking men and women in uniform with a lot of shiny stars, clearly high-ranking. When I caught her eye, she left them and came outside.

I explained about the message, and the other note, then handed them both to her.

"I'll get them sent off to check for fingerprints, but it's a long shot. They often become smudged or worn when someone else handles them."

"We didn't know what it was until we picked it up."

"I understand. Max, give me the details of the man you bought the campervan from and I'll get some people around there as soon as we've checked for fingerprints. It's best not to rush into anything until we know what we're working with."

"Okay, that sounds sensible."

"But listen, this is most likely just an idiot playing a very bad joke. The previous owner either has a bad sense of humour, or more likely someone that stayed in the camper thought it was funny. Kids maybe?"

"Maybe. I have to admit, it's rattled me. To think someone might have been held against their will in there has put a real downer on the whole thing."

"That's not the way to think about it. Whatever happened, it's history. You've given that campervan a new lease on life and it's being used for good now. Maybe that's why your calling is to help others. To make amends for something terrible that happened."

"Almost like the van wanted me to do this? A way for it to eradicate the bad memories?"

"Now you're getting carried away," she laughed. "But yes, if you like. You said this is your duty now, that you've had this feeling that it's why you took up vanlife and keep encountering these mysteries. Now you know why. The van wants to put right the wrongs that happened."

"Now you're getting carried away too," I teased.

"Maybe I am. It's been a long and exhausting few days. I want to go home and not come back. We're snowed under with trying to keep everyone safe, but however many people we bring in, it still might not be enough if the killer tries to strike again."

"You're doing your best. And at least they won't escape."

"They could easily slip away into the night like before, then leave tomorrow with everyone else. This whole thing is an utter disaster. Benny should have closed, and because he wouldn't, he should have been shut down. But we can't get it done in time, so here we are."

"Any updates?"

"No, none. What about you?"

I explained about talking to Ivan and his theory it was over beer, but Kate had heard about it from Benny and everything in the beer tent was fine. With no other news to share, we parted, both promising to keep the other updated. I was still shocked by her change of heart and how open she now was to me being involved, but with no new leads it wasn't looking good for this evening.

It was time to talk to the last few people I could think of, so I headed back down to see if Min was up for it.

As I returned, it was impossible to avoid the fact that this was a time for celebration. Whatever crazy things were going on in the world, most people were content to spend a weekend in a field with a load of strangers, sleep on the ground, use toilets they wouldn't store their lawnmower in, and get busy relaxing.

The atmosphere was contagious, and my spirits lifted. I'd had one of the best afternoons of my life resting beside Min and Anxious, and although there were certainly terrible things going on, I couldn't help but feel optimistic. Optimistic about life, my future, and that I would figure everything out. The strange notes would have to wait; there were more pressing things to deal with first.

"What are you looking so happy about?" asked Min, peering at me suspiciously as she brushed her hair. "Did Kate give you good news?"

"No, but she's having the notes checked for fingerprints."

"That's a start. She wasn't grumpy?"

"She was nice, but curt like she always is. I guess we got off to a rocky start with her, but I like her now."

"Me too. Sometimes people are rude when they feel uncomfortable and I think that's what it was with her. She didn't like being here, still doesn't, and hated that we were interfering. But she's doing her best now, and that's great."

"You all set? You look beautiful."

"Thank you." Min beamed, always pleased to receive a compliment the same as everyone else. They were free to give, so I tried to hand them out as often as possible as it made the other person happy and me feel better too.

With a spring in our step, Anxious as jubilant as a dog allowed to roam free in a field full of people keen to hand out sausages could be, and with his new jacket on to cool him down as the sun reached its zenith, we once again entered the fray.

Heavy drum and bass pounded from a large marquee, a punk band were whipping the crowd into a frenzy, the main stage had a folk singer that drew the biggest following, and the circus people were doing the rounds, throwing glitter, handing out hula-hoops, and teaching a semi-feral gaggle of children how to juggle with pretend knives. The fire-eater had made a circle of flames around which astonished festival-goers gathered as she contorted into seemingly impossible poses whilst blowing fire.

We wandered, soaking up the atmosphere, the growing anticipation for the night's festivities, the air vibrating with music and good vibes.

"Doesn't it feel wonderful?"

"It sure does. Everyone's having a great time. This is the best year yet. Apart from you know what," I added.

"Max, don't feel down. We're doing what we can and everyone's free to decide for themselves what they do. If they want to stay, that's up to them. Let's not get maudlin."

"I'm not. Honestly, I feel great. Happy. This has been so much fun. That's because we're all together."

"It has been incredible. All the food, the people, seeing Anxious so full of life, and us getting on so well. I can even picture myself living in Vee. Although it is very cramped."

"Really?" I blurted, stopping and focusing on her. "You aren't freaked out by the messages?"

"That's in the past. It's the future I'm concerned about. And I, now don't laugh, I was thinking about it when you went to find Kate, and I'm convinced this is why you've become embroiled in these mysteries. It's Vee! She wants you to help people. It's why it's your calling. You saw her, bought her, looked after her, and this is what she wants. To have someone kind living in her and to help make the world a better place."

"Min, I had the exact same feeling! I even told Kate and she agreed. I know it sounds rather wild, but it's karma, isn't it? I'm righting wrongs because of my past, but also because something happened with Vee and the camper wants to make up for what went on. Wow, this sounds crazy."

"Just because it sounds crazy, doesn't mean it isn't true." Min wagged her finger, face serious, then she cracked a smile and flung herself at me, wrapping her arms tightly around my waist then nuzzling into my chest.

The day was now officially amazing!

We said nothing when we broke apart, then it was all business. We wandered around, eyes peeled, Anxious trailing scents, and it wasn't long before he picked up on something. With a yip, he ran around us to ensure he got our attention, then he was off.

Weaving through the now thick throng, we managed to keep him in our sights as he scampered up the rise towards the beer tent. Rather than go inside, he veered off to the left and followed the trail before walking towards a fence that separated the paths leading up and down.

He only stopped when he bumped into the legs of a man I recognised. Anxious looked up, sat, and stared at him as if expecting a biscuit from the stranger who hadn't even noticed him.

Not one to give up easily, he barked a greeting, tail swishing against the dusty earth, and the man finally looked down.

We hurried over, and I congratulated Anxious then gave him a biscuit. Satisfied he'd done his job, he lay beside the fence and tucked in.

"Hi. Are you Crispin Cotteril?"

"Who's asking?" he grumbled with a frown, eyes roaming back to the beer tent.

"I'm Max, this is Min, and we wondered if we might ask you a few questions?"

"About what? Do I know you?" Crispin tugged at limp hair, his gangly frame hunched, his face covered in a sheen of sweat. He was a scruffy man, with loose, grubby, faded jeans, battered classic Adidas trainers, and a Metallica tour T-shirt from the late eighties. His beard was straggly, like he just couldn't be bothered to even look at it.

"You don't know us, no, but we've been trying to discover who killed a member of my uncle's band. And the singer last night."

"Terrible business," he sighed, wiping his forehead with the back of his hand, his eyes unable to stay focused on us and once again drifting to the beer tent.

"Was that you in the tent early this morning?" I asked, deciding to be direct.

"You what!?" he spluttered, eyes finally resting on me. "Don't know what you're talking about."

"I think you do. I saw you. You were trying to hide, but it was you."

"Fine, what if it was? What business is it of yours?"

"I'm helping the police, so is Min, and are you saying you don't mind me telling her? You have nothing to hide?"

"We just want the truth," said Min, taking a softer approach.

Crispin sank into himself even more, his hunch pronounced, and coughed into his hand. "Yeah, it was me.

But I didn't do nothing wrong. Just snoopin', seeing what the new team were up to. Benny really screwed me over and I ain't happy, but don't go trying to pin no murder on me."

"We aren't. We're just talking to everyone we can. Especially if they were acting suspicious," said Min with a warm smile.

"Yeah, well, it ain't like that. I wanted to check the set-up, see if this new lot are any good. It was a tidy operation, which gets my goat, but yeah, it was me."

"What happened between you and Benny?" I asked.

"He threw a wobbly! Reckoned I was watering down the beer and stealing the takings. He's a liar and a cheat. I'd never do that. It's my reputation on the line. He's the one who's the crook. He got offered a better deal from this new lot with their fancy micro-brewery and wanted out of our contract. He set the lawyers on me and I didn't stand a chance. He lied about the beer, messed with the books so nothing added up, and had me over a barrel. I shouldn't have come, but I've been here since the beginning. I know all the faces, all the bands, and I couldn't miss out. If you want to talk to anyone, then talk to Benny. He's the criminal in this." Crispin wiped a tear from his eye, then without a word or even a glance at us, he sloped off, looking like a man with the weight of the world on his shoulders.

"He's not a happy guy," I noted.

"Think we should talk to Benny?"

"And ask what? Did you cheat your partner out of his business and go with someone else because they were cheaper? I trust Benny. Don't you?"

"Sure, or I thought I did, but what if Crispin is telling the truth?"

"My guess is they didn't see eye to eye, so when Benny found discrepancies he took advantage to get out of the contract. But let's leave this for now and find the last person we need to speak to before I am officially out of ideas."

"You'll figure it out, Max. You always do."
"I hope you're right, because it's four already and we don't have long until the killer will most likely strike again."

Chapter 18

Campbell, the festival promoter, was not an easy man to track down. I resorted to calling Benny Nails and asking if he knew where he might be. He wasn't best pleased that Campbell was still here, but told me where to find him, so we made our way slowly to a small hidden area in the woods we didn't even know existed.

Tucked away down a path with a tiny sign pointing the way, we were instantly entombed in a living willow tunnel leading into a small clearing festooned with ribbons, flags, and bunting. A fire crackled from the centre, with stumps to sit on. Only half of them were taken, as most people were using the picnic benches or gathered over by a tiki bar. Mellow music played softly from large speakers, the vibe very chilled.

Campbell was easy to spot because he was the centre of attention. People were fawning over him like he could click his fingers and give them the future they craved. By the way he was acting, it was evident he'd had enough and was about to leave, so we decided to hang back and wait until he did exactly that.

Young musicians approached as if craving an audience with royalty, heads down, or trying to brazen it out but turning into wrecks the moment he locked his hard eyes on them. Most he dismissed with a curt word, or ignored completely, while those part of his inner circle laughed and continued to simper.

I disliked the whole scenario instantly. Young, up-and-coming musicians knew the clout he had, that if he wanted to he could get them on stage at prime times and unlock a bright future for them, but at what cost to their dignity? Was I being harsh? I realised I was, as artists poured their hearts and souls into their music and yet the business was undoubtedly cutthroat. Anyone who made it needed skill, luck, a good manager, and bundles of cash behind them if they were to turn their passion into a living.

"He's horrid," whispered Min.

"Just rather up himself by the looks of it. Maybe he's a nice guy when he's not trying to act like the big promoter."

"You think?" Min's eyebrow drifted skyward.

"No, I think we're going to have our work cut out getting him to talk. But let's give it a go anyway. Look, here he comes."

With a wave at his "friends" and a few called words, Campbell swaggered away, his movements assured and somewhat cocky. He wore plain dark jeans with a black linen shirt, the sleeves rolled up to reveal numerous bracelets and bangles, but no festival tags. Rather, he wore a lanyard like a badge of honour, and I doubted he even needed that. Average sized, with glossy raven hair that was clearly dyed, he undoubtedly had something arresting about him, but he was predatory and seemed to know it. Playing on it, rather than trying to disguise his nature.

Although judging others so quickly went against my nature, I found myself disliking him already, and wondered if the feeling in my stomach meant we had finally found our killer.

"Excuse me," said Min in her best posh voice, stepping forward to bar his progress, "do you mind if we have a quick word with you?"

Campbell stopped, looked Min up and down in a way that made my blood boil and bile rise, then leered. I don't think I'd even seen anything so disgusting in my life, and as Anxious growled I had to stop myself from doing the same thing.

"My, you're a pretty little thing, aren't you?" drooled Campbell, grinning at Min as he studied her legs.

"That's it, I can't do it!" shouted Min, turning to me and shaking her head. "He's vile. He's like a snake. Max, I'm sorry, but if I stay here a moment longer I'll batter him. Anxious, come. Leave Max to talk to this... thing!" Min flung her arms up in the air, hissed at the startled Campbell, then stomped off with Anxious chasing after her.

"She's a feisty one," laughed Campbell. "Something I said?"

"Not so much what you said, although that was gross and demeaning, as how you said it and the way you leered at her. Have you ever met someone that you adore so much you would do anything for them? A person you know is wonderful and will try your hardest to make happy?"

"Can't say I have," he snapped. "Who are you?"

"Let me finish," I warned. "That woman you leered at and demeaned is the love of my life. Even if she was a complete stranger, it wouldn't matter. What is wrong with you? You can't behave like that. You're a grown man and you should know better. Just because you get people sucking up to you, doesn't mean everyone thinks you're great. They just want something from you, Campbell. They don't care about you or even like you. You've been at this game too long if you think for one moment that's an appropriate way to act. Shame on you." I sucked in air after my tirade, relaxed my hands bunched into tight fists, and had to forcibly calm myself and let my shoulders lower. "Oh, I'm Max," I added.

Campbell's mouth opened and closed but no words came out, his neck flushed, but then the strangest thing happened. He smiled. A genuine, warm, happy smile.

"Max, I'm so sorry. You're right, and I knew it even as I acted that way. Come over here. You and I need to talk."

With a nod, Campbell led me to a picnic bench tucked away under the trees. He glared at the people already approaching, warning them to back off, and we were left alone.

We sat opposite each other, and he wasted no time talking. "You're the only person in years who has spoken to me so honestly. Everyone wants something from me, and I guess I've become quite a monster. I didn't mean to, but I guess I let the power go to my head. I apologise. And please apologise to that woman. Your wife?"

"It's complicated. Um, I wasn't expecting this."

"Neither was I," he chuckled, shaking his head. "Now that you have my attention, what do you want? You aren't a musician are you?" he asked warily.

"No. I wanted to talk to you about the murders. I'm helping to solve them, and I'm getting close. To be blunt, I wanted to sound you out and see if I thought you orchestrated this whole thing."

"Don't be a clown, Max. Why would I do that?"

"To ruin Benny's name so you could swoop in and take the festival off his hands?"

"That's not how I do business. Benny made it clear he doesn't want to sell, and that's fine by me. I have more than enough on my plate. There are no hard feelings beyond my pride being hurt. As I'm sure you've noticed, I usually get what I want. People don't say no to Campbell."

"I already figured that out. Let me ask you another question then."

"Shoot." He actually made a gun with his fingers and a clicking sound, so he still wasn't that great a guy.

"What's your take on the whole thing?"

"Hmm, let me think." He stroked his chin as if deep in thought, then laughed and admitted, "It's got me stumped. There are no end of shady characters, as I'm sure you know. I've heard about you, and your ex, and the dog, so sorry for pretending I didn't know who you were, but there's a long list of suspects. Your uncle and his band members. Benny.

The Third Skatallion as they hated their lead singer. Then we have the issues over the beer tent and Benny and Crispy falling out. There's the outright warfare over the stands and the bickering about who gets to play when, and some of the security are suspect too. The circus people are always grumbling about being left out and not given enough space to perform, or enough money, the fire-eater had a big fight with Benny the other day about lax safety measures, and Ivan and the others from his band are hanging in there by the skin of their teeth and angry about not being allowed to get the prime merchandise spot, no matter what Ivan might have told you."

"You know a lot about what goes on around here," I said, impressed.

"It's my job to know, and people tell me all sorts to get into my good books. But the problem is, this is just the usual nonsense that goes on at events. You think this is wild? This is small potatoes. You should hear what goes on at the big festivals. You wouldn't believe me if I told you."

"Then you can keep that to yourself," I laughed. "What's your gut telling you? If you've been around the festival circuit so long, and none of the intrigue surprises you, what's your take on it all?"

"That whoever the murderer is, they're pretty smart. They haven't stuck to one means of killing, they can blend in as there are so many people, and they are definitely going to go for Ivan and his crew tonight. Good luck with it, Max. I've already warned Ivan, but he's adamant they're playing. That's on him."

"Thanks, and I might owe you an apology, but I won't give one. I'm pleased you apologised for how you acted, but I'm guessing you'll jump straight back into being the old Campbell, right?"

"Everyone expects it of me now," he sighed, looking beaten down and stressed for a moment before the scowl was locked back in place. "I'm a lost cause. I don't think I know how to act any other way."

"You can always try. See how you feel. You've been nice enough to me. Maybe give that a shot with others?"

"Maybe. Good luck, Max, because you're gonna need it."

"I think maybe you need it more than me, Campbell." I stood and left him staring off into space.

I found Min and Anxious waiting at the edge of the woods. After explaining what had happened, and her calming down, we returned to the campervan for a much needed rest. I lasted five seconds then put dinner on, the calming act of cooking letting everything filter through my overheating head until things finally began to click into place.

Once I'd put the pot on low to simmer, I sat beside Min and we talked everything through, leaving nobody, and nothing, out. When I explained my reasoning for my suspicions, she couldn't believe we'd overlooked it, and became very animated.

"We have to tell the cops. Get the detective here. Kate Moss, and I wish she wasn't called that as I keep expecting her to do a fancy walk and say a cheesy line about the London look, should know."

"I'll call her and explain what we think is happening, but I doubt she'll do anything but keep an eye on our suspect."

"Do you really think they'll risk another killing tonight?"

"I'm convinced they will. This isn't over yet. Two killings haven't had the desired effect, so it's got to be three. We need to make sure that doesn't happen. He'll go for Ivan, and won't back down, so we need to stop this before it's curtains for your boyfriend."

"We can't let Ivan die. He's the best," whimpered Min, rubbing her red eyes.

"Don't you worry, I'll do my best to save the love of your life." I said it with a smile, but my words must have conveyed the bitter undertone even though I knew Min didn't feel that way.

"Max, you know it's just a rock star crush, don't you? Not a real love. Not like..."

"I know. I was only teasing. Sorry to sound jealous. I mean, he is a hunk."

"Isn't he? So handsome and rugged. And that long hair and the way he leaves his shirt button undone. It's just so cool."

I went to check on dinner and get everything ready while Min wiped away the drool.

It took her a while, so I made a few calls, explained to Kate what had been happening, and she was surprisingly upbeat about it. She thanked me, said she'd put everything in place, and then I called Moose and Uncle Ernie.

They both arrived an hour later when dinner was almost ready, so Min and I gave our guests a drink, we chatted about the day we'd had, and with no new insights from Moose who'd been busy on patrol but with no big revelations, I got down to the serious business of explaining who the murderer was.

Ernie took it as read that I was right, Moose needed more convincing.

Once dinner was served, and everyone tucked in, with Anxious getting a generous portion as we were going to have a busy night, we formulated our plan. After we'd eaten, and Moose had finished his third helping, he left to begin the preparations for what would either see us revealing the killer, or us being responsible for ensuring he not only committed another murder but got away with it. The risk was huge, but I could think of no other way to actually prove who it was.

With the dishes done, and everything cleared away, Ernie, Min, Anxious, and I headed up to the arena to listen to awesome bands, join the record numbers for the last night, and stop a rock god being murdered in front of thousands of adoring fans. One in particular would be distraught if he died tonight.

Chapter 19

The line to enter the main arena was long. Nobody was taking any chances, so bags and pockets were being checked thoroughly by a veritable army of security and police. There were grumbles from the keen music fans, but the line moved quickly and soon enough we were through.

As we shuffled along with everyone else, I repeatedly saw a dark figure weaving in and out of the throng, here one minute, gone the next. Moose was in full ninja mode and as stealthy as a black cat on a moonless night.

Excited voices and pounding music battered our eardrums from all directions, but Anxious had his ear mufflers on so trotted along happily until the crowds got too dense and Min carried him.

"Exciting, isn't it, eh?" asked Uncle Ernie, tipping his trilby back and pinging his black braces. He looked very smart with a clean white polo shirt and a fresh pair of dark drainpipe trousers.

"It really is," I admitted, my heart beating fast, my temperature rising as bodies brushed against us.

"I can't wait to see how everyone does this evening. I'm so looking forward to seeing Danger to Life," gushed Min.

"Don't forget our plan," I reminded her.

"How could I? But I'm still going to enjoy them. They'll be awesome."

"Aye, they're a fine band," agreed Ernie. "Ivan's a real superstar. Shame he hasn't got my looks, or they could have gone far."

Min and I stared at my rangy, rather wrinkly uncle with his trousers hitched up revealing orange socks, and Doc Marten shoes.

"Yes, Uncle," I chuckled, "he could have made it big if he looked like you."

"Been properly famous," tittered Min.

"They did alright," said Uncle Ernie, then burst out laughing.

"Since when do you wear orange socks?" I asked. "It's always white, isn't it?"

"Fancied a change. And I, er, had to borrow a pair from Stu as I was out of clean ones."

Min and I exchanged a look, but said nothing more.

We stopped at the beer tent first and got a drink where it was quieter while an act played, then went back down to the other stage to watch a raucous punk band give it all they had. We went wild in the mosh pit while Anxious waited at the back of the audience. It felt good to let loose and burn off the pent-up energy.

I lost myself to the music, all thoughts and concerns forgotten as the beats took over, the drums pounding through my veins. Min and I staggered away after a few songs, exhausted and smiling, and watched the rest of the set with Anxious while Ernie pogoed and skanked like a pro.

After that, we moved up to the main stage and readied for the penultimate act of the night. The crowds were gathered in force now, keening for a real showstopper. Word had got out, and nobody wanted to miss what might be the show of a lifetime, in more ways than one. I felt certain that tonight it would be during Danger to

Life's performance that the killer would attack again. It was simply too good an opportunity for them to miss.

Nevertheless, I felt nervous, and so did Min judging by the way she kept squeezing my hand and glancing at me.

The band came on to the stage looking apprehensive, studying the expectant faces, then took their positions before the lead singer said hello to raucous cheers. Grinning, he asked if he could please not be killed, eliciting a roar of laughter.

Then the lights went out, everyone gasped, the band struck, and the party got started. They played an incredible set, each track louder, faster, more energetic than the last, but as the frontman sang his last note and the guitars died, they couldn't get off the stage fast enough.

The crowd called for an encore, but instead Benny Nails appeared on stage wearing army fatigues, a helmet, and what looked like a bullet-proof vest. Everyone cheered and laughed, entranced by the drama, as Benny waved then took the mike.

"Thank you for coming!" he hollered to applause. "Nobody's going to spoil our fun, right?" Revellers roared their agreement. "But Benny Nails is taking no chances. Like my helmet?" Everyone laughed and hollered encouragement. "Be careful out there, and if you see anything suspicious report it to the police or the security staff. This event is really special to all of us, so let's have a great time. Are you ready?" Thousands cheered. "I said, are you ready?" The noise levels rose as everyone shouted until they were hoarse. "Then please welcome Danger to Life!" Benny handed the mike to Ivan as he strutted across the stage.

Thousands of people erupted into an eardrum-piercing cheer as Ivan flung his hair over his shoulders, undid another button, causing half the audience to gasp, the other half to groan, and began belting out the first track as the band give it all they had.

The lights turned off as the smoke machines belched, then a riot of colour strobed across the densely-packed revellers as the guys in the engineers' booth worked their magic. Timed to perfection, the lighting pulsed to the beats of the old rockers, and when the first track ended the applause was as deafening as the song itself.

The second track was a more mellow affair, Ivan's vocals at the fore. He still had an incredible voice, and it truly had improved with age. The guitars wailed, the drums beat steadily, and the bass pulsed as the older generation swayed and the younger ones readied for the wild times we knew were coming.

Song three upped the tempo, and most were dancing as they sang along to a familiar classic the band must have played thousands of times. But it didn't show, and they played their hearts out, whipping up a storm as lights flashed across a sea of blissful faces. Everyone was lost to the music and atmosphere as thousands of people came together in a field to have a good time and forget about the outside world.

Why would anyone want to spoil that? Regretfully, I knew, and it saddened me no end, but we'd get what justice we could, and hopefully this would go off without anyone getting hurt.

Song after song improved on the last, the atmosphere now so tense you could cut it with a knife. Min and I moved back up to the side of the booth, with Uncle Ernie having made his way to the path where he could gain access to backstage.

"Where's Moose?" shouted Min in my ear, her words still little but a whisper above the incredible guitars screeching from the speakers.

"There." I pointed at a dark shadow several feet away, but when Min turned he was gone.

"I don't see him."

"Over there now," I said, pointing again.

"How does he do that?" she gasped as we caught a flash of his face when the lights brightened, before he vanished.

"I have no idea. Are you ready for this? It'll be the last song, right at the end, or maybe after."

"I'm ready. And aren't they amazing? This is the best they've ever played, and they've never done a bad set."

"They're incredible," I admitted. "Think how stressed they must be, but they're still going for it."

We moved away. Lost to the dark, nothing but the dimmed overhead lights by the beer tent to light our way. It was enough to see by, but easy enough to hide with so many shadows and the lights from the stage alternately blinding you then plunging everything into darkness.

The police presence was strong, the same as private security, but they were absolutely swamped by the sheer volume of people. Bodies pressed against each other everywhere you went, with the approach to the beer tent particularly congested. We took a circuitous route away from the crowds so Anxious didn't get lost, and came up by the cabin for the staff.

"See anything?" asked Moose, startling us as he appeared from nowhere.

"Eek," Min squealed, then smiled as she giggled. "You have to teach me that."

"There's nothing to it," shrugged our gentle giant of a new friend.

"We haven't seen anything yet. I don't think we will until the very end. What about you?" I asked.

"Very quiet, but everyone's ready. Won't be long now. Although, it would be better if nothing happened at all."

"That would be the ideal outcome, but we also need to catch them in the act so they can never do something like this again." I noted Uncle Ernie weaving through the dense throng, heading to the beer tent, hand on his hat so he didn't lose it. He caught my eye and winked before going to order a drink. His orange socks flashed as the lights picked up the excited faces of people sipping on cool drinks, the humidity clearly high under so much plastic.

The remaining members of The Third Skatallion were grouped together, none of them looking overly happy, probably because they weren't currently selling any T-shirts. Campbell was the centre of attention as usual, but he was ignoring everyone and focusing on the band. Even Crispin, Benny's disgruntled ex-partner, was having a drink, face sour, clearly lamenting the money he'd lost.

All the people we'd questioned were seen over the next few songs. Even the fire-eater in her sparkly costume was drinking pint after pint, which I guess you'd be grateful for after burning your face and throat repeatedly for days. I spied the circus crowd, some in costume, others in regular clothes. Children gathered around the young tightrope walker who was blowing bubbles using a machine, sending the kids and several dogs racing after them towards the big top.

Jordan Flanagan, the man I'd spied in the cabin sleeping off a heavy night was standing like a statue up by the Jamaican food stall, watching every move the customers made, and more security were stationed at every other stall.

People came and went, tired but happy, before new faces took their place. It was a dizzying experience trying to keep an eye on everyone, and I found it difficult not to focus on our suspect, but now was not the time to give the game away.

Ivan spoke to the crowd after a song ended, explaining this was to be their last track. Now beyond excited not only for the finale, but because the killer had yet to strike, the entire festival erupted in a roar of encouragement, and Ivan wasted no time counting down.

On three, the entire site was plunged into darkness, then the band struck, the lights flared, and everyone went absolutely crazy. It was a set like no other, with band, engineers, and fans holding nothing back.

We remained in position, watching carefully, knowing now wasn't the time. I caught the eye of many familiar faces, but did nothing but smile then look away, keen to avoid them getting suspicious.

The last track finished, the lights faded, and cheers vibrated the site, calling for an encore. The curtains closed, then a wail rose in pitch from a guitar. A lone chord singing out across the site and the hills beyond.

And then the curtain opened, fireworks lit up the sky, and the spotlight hit Ivan as the band played their instruments like their lives depended on it. Ivan held the mike two-handed, screaming out the lyrics to their most popular song ever, and yet he could barely be heard above the excited shouts of the people as they danced and smiled.

The tension was palpable; everyone knew there was something coming. Would the killer really risk striking again? I knew they would.

As the song finished with a final beat of a drum, the place erupted with applause. The lights went out once more as more fireworks exploded overhead, then a single spotlight focused on Ivan, making him the absolute centre of attention.

I counted down in my head.

Three.

Two.

One.

With perfect timing, Ivan ducked aside as the spotlight shone as bright as day and tracked across the field, highlighting Bonbon in full clown costume up on the bank. At least three feet taller than anyone else, he stood expertly on his stilts, his bow raised and arrow notched.

"Now," I told Min and Anxious, then hurriedly jabbed at my phone, sending the message to everyone I'd already been in contact with.

Bonbon's green hair shone brightly as the red-nosed clown teetered, the light disorienting him, then he threw away the bow, let the arrow drop, and jumped from the stilts, looking around in a panic.

Ernie, DS Kate, her entourage of uniformed officers, and several security converged on Bonbon, aka Brian, as he shoved through the crowd, the lights following as he flung his wig aside. He batted at people, slid between confused fans, then vanished.

Min and I chased after Anxious as he tore after Bonbon, catching up with him in seconds as the shocked crowd stayed put, waiting for this to play out, unable to believe this was real and that everything they'd been told was true.

Anxious barked then tore off again; we found him with the green wig in his mouth, shaking it fiercely.

"I think it's dead, Anxious. Go find Bonbon."

He dropped the wig, then chased off towards the backstage access.

With the lights strobing over people's heads, searching for Bonbon, it was easy to see our way, and I knew this wasn't over yet. Brian was not about to give up, the clown Bonbon alter-ego now discarded as I trampled over a pair of colourful trousers and a sparkly, glitter-covered waistcoat.

"He's going after Ivan. They're still on the stage," I told Min.

"Then let's save the god of rock," she panted as we skidded to a halt outside the backstage access, the security rushing inside, leaving us free to enter.

Anxious led the way, checking we were following, and we raced past stored equipment then burst onto the stage.

"Stop!" I bellowed as Brian, now looking just like a regular festival-goer with a painted face but everyday clothes, walked casually between the security, holding a bundle of wires like he worked there, heading straight for Ivan.

"It's him. Stop that evil clown!" ordered Min, then turned to me and grinned. "I've always wanted to say that."

"You have?" I asked, then grabbed her hand and said, "Come on."

Brian turned at the commotion as we raced forward. Anxious barked, the security converged, and DS Kate Moss stepped out of the shadows on the other side of the stage with two officers beside her.

"Who are you?" shouted Ivan as Brian stopped dead in his tracks, eyes darting around the stage.

"You... you don't even know, do you? You make me sick!"

Suddenly, the curtains drew back, the lights clicked loudly as the entire stage was flooded with red light, and the crowd still amassed gasped as the sound boomed out from the speakers for all to hear.

"You were going to kill me?" shouted Ivan, his gravelly voice eliciting a wave of sighs and gasps from the crowd before silence descended, everyone keening to hear the ultimate encore of their lives.

"You deserve it. How did you know? There's no way you could have known it was me," he roared, looking from Ivan, to Kate Moss, then to Min, Anxious, and me as we approached warily.

"I figured it out because you weren't quite as smart as you thought you were," I said, shielding my eyes against the glare, shocked to hear my voice bouncing back at me from the speakers.

"You! The man asking all the questions. Max Effort, the wannabe detective. I was certain I had you fooled. Nobody could have known it was me."

"I did. You killed Dutch and you shot Major Two-Tone, but you didn't care about them. You just cared about Ivan."

The crowd oohed and aahed, caught up in the drama. A show like no other, full of famous rock stars, stunned guitarists, amazed bass players, a little dog sitting and wagging happily, wondering if there would be biscuits, and numerous nervous police officers.

"I had to make it look like it was someone wanting to disrupt the festival," spat Brian. "I'm sorry they had to die, but it was the only way."

"You could have not killed anyone," said Min.

"No, it had to be done."

"But you were lax. I checked the spot where I thought you'd fired the arrow, but there was no sign of anyone having been there. But just beside the cabin we found glitter. A lot of glitter. You're always covered in it. You dropped it when you changed out of your clown costume. Nobody would recognise you without it, and the kids would leave you alone. You used your stilts to shoot Major Two-Tone, and you gave yourself away."

"That's a lie. You couldn't figure it out that way."

"I think we've heard enough," snapped Kate Moss. "You are under arrest for—"

"Ivan must die!" Brian lunged for Ivan as the entire site held its collective breath, but he dodged aside and the police hurried to apprehend the disgruntled clown.

He raced around the stage, narrowly avoiding capture, then turned, sneered at me, and smiled as he raced towards the front of the stage and dove off.

Chapter 20

Delighted fans roared as Bonbon hit the hands of the cheering masses and he rode the tide on his back, carried away from the stage.

"What are you waiting for?" snapped Kate Moss, her curt words amplified for all to hear.

The officers looked from her to the sea of expectant faces, and shrugged. They dove off the stage, but seemingly it was not to be, as neither launched past the barriers and landed flat on their faces, groaning in pain.

"We'll get him," came a voice from between me and Min as Moose appeared.

As Anxious barked a hello, Moose smiled then grabbed our arms and thundered forward, leaving us no choice but to be dragged along.

Anxious whined, then yipped with delight as he sprinted between Moose's sturdy legs and sprang into the delighted audience. He was caught instantly, and directed towards Bonbon, passed from one set of sweaty hands to the next.

"Make sure you bend your legs," I shouted to Min as Moose launched over the barriers, releasing our hands as we sailed towards our fate.

I landed with a surprisingly gentle bump onto the heads and hands of everyone, then was instantly crowd-surfing.

"That way, after the killer," I shouted, and smiling faces nodded as I angled to the right and was handed over time and time again. Min passed me by, wailing but smiling as we locked eyes. Then Moose swept past, his huge bulk seemingly no concern to the loyal fans of Lydstock. Like a leaf on a fast-running stream, he glided along on the ever-changing surface.

I rolled onto my belly and gasped as Moose somehow got to his feet and raced across the upturned palms as though his feet weren't even touching. A feather clad in black, he was weightless as he surged ahead then dove like a pro rugby player at Bonbon and grabbed him in an iron-fisted tackle. Both disappeared from sight.

I caught up with Min and asked the flock of rock fans to let us down, then Anxious barked happily as he glided past before he, too, vanished.

We hurried through the parting onlookers, nobody wanting to get in our way, everyone spreading out to form a circle impossible to escape from as we approached Moose and Bonbon.

We emerged into what felt like a fighting arena of old, the press of bodies tight, faces excited but concerned as Moose and Bonbon squared off against each other. Bonbon, although I guess now he was just plain Brian, had a knife in his hand and a wicked leer on his face.

Anxious emerged and trotted over to us happily, yipping away, telling of his adventure, so I ruffled his fur and told him how brave he was, then moved forward to help Moose.

"I got this," said Moose softly. "Don't risk getting stabbed."

"I can't leave you to handle him alone," I protested.

Moose winked, then said, "Don't you worry about me."

"You ruined everything," accused Brian, then with a roar, eliciting a gasp from the swarm, he raced towards me, knife held high.

Moose vanished, one moment there, the next gone. Anxious launched, then tore at Brian's ankle, doing what he did best. The twisted clown stumbled, but he was almost upon me, so I moved away from Min to ensure she was safe, then readied to defend myself.

With Anxious hanging off his shin now, Brian roared in undisguised hatred and brought his hand down, ready to end my life.

"You missing something?" I asked, smiling as I nodded to Moose, who had somehow appeared behind him and snatched the knife without Brian even realising.

As Brian's arm lowered, I chopped out at his elbow and something cracked. As the murderous clown howled in pain, Anxious took the opportunity to drag backwards, causing Brian to lose his footing and crash to the ground.

We stood over him as he squirmed. Uncle Ernie appeared, dropping down from tired hands, and gasped, "Best crowd-surfing ever!" then beamed at us. "Did we get him?"

"We got him," I said, nodding to Brian.

"What's this all about, you utter maniac?" demanded Uncle Ernie.

"You broke my arm," wailed Brian as he clambered awkwardly to his feet now Anxious had released him.

"You deserve worse than that," snarled Benny Nails as people gave him space to join us. "What made you do it, Brian? How could you? You murdered two people and almost killed a third. Ivan's an utter god. Are you out of your mind?"

"I had to. It was the only way to ensure I got away with it tonight. I planned it so everyone would think it was some nutter trying to put an end to the festival, but I knew you'd never close the place down. Still as greedy as always."

"Greedy? I pay you good wages, and you come year after year."

"This wasn't about money anyway," mumbled Brian, the crowd pressing close to us now, not wanting to miss a word.

"What was it about then?" asked Benny with a frown.

"I think I know," I said.

"What?" enquired several thousand people.

"Ivan."

"Ivan?" everyone asked.

"Yes, I understand now. I saw it the moment you appeared on stage," said Ivan as he entered the clearing.

"Tell us!" everyone roared.

"He's your son, isn't he?" I asked.

"I think so." Ivan turned to Brian. "Are you my son?"

"Of course I am. I look just like you! But you never cared, did you? You never looked after me or Mum. You abandoned us."

"I never even knew you existed," said Ivan softly.

"Well, you do now. How does it feel, eh, to know you're responsible for two people being dead?" sneered Brian.

"That's on you, not Ivan," I said. "Why didn't you reach out to him if you knew he was your father?"

"Because he never tried to help us. He's no real father of mine."

"But I was never told," protested Ivan. "Sure, I was rather wild when I was younger, but I'd never abandon my own flesh and blood."

"Liar!" Brian lunged for Ivan, but the police finally appeared and subdued him.

The lighting, which I hadn't even realised was still focused on us, changed from reds to greens, then began to flash, and music blared from speakers as Brian was led away.

"How about an encore?" pleaded a man as he stepped into the fast-closing space.

"Yes, encore!" everyone shouted.

"I think you better," I told a confused and clearly distraught Ivan.

"One song," he shouted, much to everyone's delight.

We pushed through the excited people and away up the path to the almost empty beer tent. I wasn't surprised to find Moose and Kate Moss there with Benny Nails and Uncle Ernie, along with a few other band members and some from The Third Skatallion.

Brian was being read his rights as Danger to Life cranked out one last song, the entire festival delighting in the unexpected encore and the extreme drama.

Nobody moved until the band finished and Ivan approached. Festival-goers knew this was now a private matter, so turned their attention to the serious business of spending what remaining money they had in the beer tent.

Kate Moss and the officers led everyone over to the grubby cabin and we entered.

"I had to play the last song. They deserved it," said Ivan, looking distraught as he moved closer to Brian.

"Careful," warned Kate. "Give him some room."

"He's in handcuffs. What can he do?" Ivan turned back to Brian and asked, "Why try to kill me rather than talk?"

"Because you're a womaniser and a terrible person. I wanted to ruin the festival and destroy your career, and ensure you never got to let anyone down ever again."

"Why would ruining the festival matter to you?" asked Ivan.

"Because Benny never pays enough, and we're always the last to be told anything. I'd just had enough of it. You musicians think you're so much better than us. I wanted to teach you a lesson."

"You've got real issues. I'm sorry you felt abandoned, but I never knew about you. I promise. Your mum told you I was the father? Are you sure?"

"Of course I'm sure. No, she never said, but she died a few years ago. I've known for a long time it was you, and took my time planning this."

"How did you know?" I asked.

"Because we look the same. It's that simple. He's my father."

"I don't know if I am or not, but look what you've done. Taken two lives and ruined your own."

"I don't care!"

Struggling, he was taken away. Ivan went with Kate and the officers, still trying to get information from Brian. Benny was called to help out at the bar. Min, Anxious, Moose, Uncle Ernie, and I remained in the smelly room.

"Blimey, that was... Wild!" beamed Uncle Ernie, removing his trilby and wiping his sweaty forehead.

"Moose, you were amazing," gushed Min as she hugged the startled man.

"Thanks," he shrugged. "But it was no biggie."

"It was absolutely incredible." I shook his hand then went in for a hug and back pat. "How did you move across the crowd like that?"

"It was easy. Just what I do." Moose smiled, then said, "It's done."

Anxious barked, so we congratulated him. When we looked up a moment later, Moose was gone.

"How did he do that?" asked Uncle Ernie. "The door's still closed."

"Come on, let's go have a beer. I think we deserve one," I suggested.

Anxious barked.

"Yes, and a biscuit for you."

I opened the door and we stepped out into the night. The last evening of the festival had been like no other, and I prayed it never would be again.

There remained plenty of unanswered questions, but I knew that tomorrow was a new day and with it would come plenty of information once things had settled down.

For once, Uncle Ernie put his hand in his pocket and offered to buy the drinks, but he didn't even get the chance. The moment we entered the beer tent, the whole place erupted, and before we knew it, we were once more crowd-surfing. Held aloft, then deposited at the bar where everyone stepped aside.

"What'll it be?" asked Benny Nails, beaming at us from behind the bar. "It's on the house."

"Thanks, Benny. You okay? That was a shock for everyone."

"I'm great! You figured it out, caught the killer, and made the twenty-fifth anniversary Lydstock one to remember."

"Are you going to tell us the secret?" asked Min. "I think we deserve to know why it's called Lydstock, don't you?"

"You finally get me to reveal it," laughed Benny. He leaned forward and whispered, "I couldn't think of a name for the festival, so ended up just picking the first two things I saw in the kitchen. A lid, and stock for gravy. I combined them, changed the spelling, and the festival was born." Benny winked, then began pulling pints.

Min and I groaned, then shrugged. At least we had an answer to the mystery that had bugged us for years.

With our drinks, we gratefully took a picnic bench offered to us and settled down. Anxious hid under the table, munching happily on a biscuit.

"So, what's next?" asked Uncle Ernie, beaming.

"How'd you mean?" I sipped my cold beer, the adrenaline slowly dissipating.

"I mean, what's your next adventure going to be?"

"I think I've had enough adventures to last me a lifetime," I said, unable to hide my grin.

"Give him a few days, then he'll be calling me up, telling me there's been another murder," teased Min.

"I will not!"

"You will."

"Maybe," I admitted. "But let's see what tomorrow brings first. Don't forget, Kate promised to fast track getting the notes checked."

"What's this?" asked Uncle Ernie.

We explained about the messages we'd found, and the first thing he said was, "That campervan of yours is trying to right the wrongs inflicted on it. This is why you keep getting embroiled in mysteries, Max. It's to help the van feel good about itself again."

"That's what we both said, and even Kate Moss agrees," said Min.

"Uncle Ernie is always right," he said with a smile that slowly dissolved, leaving him serious and wiping his eyes. "Poor Dutch. That kid didn't deserve what happened to him. At least the killer got what he deserved, but what was that idiot thinking? I still don't understand."

"He had a beef with Benny so wanted to ruin the festival, but mostly it was to make his killing of Ivan suitably dramatic. He's obviously not well, and believes Ivan's his father. Time will tell, but I'm not so sure he's even right."

"I guess we'll find out."

"I'm sure we will," I agreed.

An hour later, we parted ways with Uncle Ernie and the three of us were locked up safe and sound in Vee. I don't think we moved until the next morning when there was a knock at the van.

Groggy, I stumbled about in the cramped space, peered through the window, then unlocked Vee and stepped outside into another beautifully hot and bright morning.

"What time is it?" I asked a sprightly-looking Kate.

"It's almost eleven. Don't tell me you were still sleeping? You lucky thing. I didn't get a wink of sleep."

"Sorry to hear that," I said with a yawn.

"Not to worry, it's over now. The paperwork is done, and I have good news."

"Really? Have you seen Moose? He vanished last night and didn't come for a drink."

"Morning," said Min as she joined us outside.

"We slept until eleven," I told her with a grin.

"Wow. I haven't done that in years."

"I was just asking if Kate had seen Moose."

"Who is this Moose?" asked Kate with a frown.

"You know, the big guy who moves like a ninja and helped us out last night."

"Very funny. Are you still half asleep?" asked Kate.

Min and I exchanged a look, then Min asked, "You don't remember him? The security guard? Went by the name Moose. He crowd-surfed, then took the knife off Brian."

"I thought that was one of my officers? But never mind that. I have information I thought you'd like to hear. I've already spoken to Ivan, but wanted to tell you what I knew about the killer and the other thing too."

I quickly set up the chairs, gave Anxious his breakfast as he began to pine, and made a coffee. Nobody spoke until it was ready, then we settled and Kate began.

"Brian is not Ivan's son. He's had several warnings and a few restraining orders over the years for stalking people he believed were his dad. The poor man has issues, so will get the help he needs."

"How do you know?" I asked.

"We ran DNA tests. There's no match. They look alike, but that's it."

"Poor Brian must be a very confused man," said Min.

"He really is. He just wanted to get revenge, but he did wrong and will spend a long time incarcerated."

"Thanks for letting us know. What's the other news?"

"There are no fingerprints on the notes you gave me. Just a few smudges apart from your own prints. It's a no-go in that regard. We've had officers around to the address you gave us, but it's a dead end too."

"He wouldn't talk? Or has he moved?"

"The previous owner died almost a month ago. Just after he sold you the van. His wife allowed the officers to search the premises, and was very helpful, apparently, but there's no sign of anything untoward. If I had to hazard a guess, I'd say this is either his, or someone else's, idea of a very bad joke."

"That's an awful thing to do," said Min. "How horrid."

"I'm sorry, but this is also good news. There are no missing persons from the area, and the previous owner's record is squeaky clean. He was a hard-working man who adored campervans. He and his wife travelled almost every weekend. He hardly ever went away alone, so it seems like he had no opportunity to have had someone locked up for weeks. It's a hoax."

"That's a real relief," I sighed, stifling a smile although I felt like cheering. "Nobody's been taken against their will, and although it's a terrible joke to play, at least we don't have to worry."

"Exactly. You can relax. Your work here is done, everyone's very grateful, and I hate to admit this," Kate smiled awkwardly, "but I had a good time. I know that's a mean thing to say when a poor, misguided man lost his way so badly he committed murder, but after you crowd-surfed, I jumped off the stage too. I actually stage-dived! I never, ever thought I'd say this, but I enjoyed the festival. Maybe I'll catch you two here next year?"

Anxious barked and rubbed against Kate's leg, seemingly having taken to her at last.

"Yes, and you, Anxious," she laughed, stroking his back.

"Maybe you will," I said.

"And maybe it will be a nice, relaxing time like it used to be," said Min.

Kate left with her usual curt nod.

"Shall I make a fry-up?" asked Min.

My heart froze, Anxious whimpered then ran for cover under the campervan, and Min laughed.

"Um..." I stammered.

"I was only joking. Let's just finish our coffee then take you know who for a you know what."

"Great idea."

We met up with several people later that morning, but it was the strangest thing. Nobody apart from me, Min, and Uncle Ernie had ever heard of a man named Moose or anyone matching his description.

It was as though he'd never existed.

Maybe he was a ninja.

"What are you smiling at?" asked Min that afternoon when everything was packed away and she was about to head off.

I'd wait until everyone else had left, to avoid the queue, and it would give me time to figure out where I was going next. I'd been so excited about the festival and Min coming that I hadn't given it a thought.

"I'm happy."

"And so am I. Don't forget, Max. Give me a call the next time there's a murder. I might not be able to come and help, but I'll certainly be there for you in any other way I can."

"Who's to say there will be another mystery?"

We laughed as the sun shone brightly on a day I wished would never end. But there would be other days, and plenty of time to enjoy life. And maybe this was the end of my manic spree solving murder mysteries.

Or maybe it was just the beginning...

The End

But you know it isn't really. Read on for a delicious one-pot wonder and news about the next adventure. Stewed to the Bone is one of Max's most grisly adventures yet, and it begins with a very peculiar set of circumstances. That's not all. Max is determined to uncover the truth about what happened in Vee. Were the notes they found hidden away really just a joke, or did something truly sinister happen in his home?

First, let's cook!

Recipe

Jamaican Jerk Chicken with Rice

I'm not saying a glass of beer or a cheeky Prosecco is a requisite for this recipe, but for those who like the fizz it certainly pairs well. Something to take the edge off this fiery dish, although feel free to amend the heat levels to suit your taste buds.

In the UK, music festivals are a great opportunity to sample cuisine from around the world, with a definite bias towards Asian, Caribbean, and the obligatory wood-fired pizza offerings. No longer just about chips and mushy peas, you get to sample plenty of options, although we do limits ourselves to one night of buying out and prefer to cook ourselves for the rest of the time. Unlike Max, we've found that the ideal approach is to bring frozen meals from batch cooking at home, and cozido de grão, the recipe from book one, is a stalwart of our festival stay.

Something spicy is always welcome, though, and when in party mood it seems to hit the spot like nothing else. Load up on rice, make enough for the next day, then reheat everything until piping hot and you have yourself a stunning lunch before the afternoon bands rouse you from your festival lethargy.

Firstly, apologies to any Jamaican jerk aficionados. This is British kitchen-based cooking—not entirely authentic, but none the worse for it. Spicy, vibrant, and very moreish. We make this most often with the chicken in the oven, and the rice on the cooker top. Here's the modified version for campfire or campervan one-pot cooking...

Ingredients

For the jerk seasoning:
- Olive oil - 1 tbsp

- Three shallots - finely chopped
- Dried thyme - 2 tsp
- Allspice - 1 tsp
- Nutmeg - grated - 1/2 tsp
- Cinnamon - 1/4 tsp
- Chilli flakes - 1 tsp
- One Scotch bonnet pepper - finely diced
- Worcestershire (or light soy) sauce - 1 tbsp
- Caster sugar - 1 tsp
- Ground black pepper - 2 tsp

For the rice:
- Basmati rice - 1 mug
- One small onion - finely chopped
- One carrot - diced
- Allspice - 1/2 tsp
- Dried thyme - 1 tsp
- Creamed coconut - 50g grated
- Kidney beans - 1 can rinsed and drained
- Vegetable or chicken stock - 2 mugs worth (made with a good cube is fine)

To cook:
- Olive oil - 2 tbsp
- Eight chicken pieces on the bone (legs / quarters / or a whole jointed chicken)
- Beer - a small glass

Method

For a one-pot treat, grab your largest flame-proof casserole/Dutch oven and prepare to sneeze...

- First of all make the seasoning by mixing the ingredients well. Ideally using a mini food processor, but if you're camping or would prefer less washing up, just chop everything tiny and mix in a bowl. Alternatively, you can cheat— Walkerswood do a fabulous Jerk seasoning that is crazy good. Use half the amount you think you'll need. It's got a kick!
- Cut a few slits in your chicken skin and rub all over with the seasoning. You could leave this in the fridge for an hour to permeate or just get on with cooking.
- Heat 2 tbsp of oil in the pot on a high heat and then brown (or blacken) the chicken all over. Do this in batches if necessary.
- Add the chicken back to the pot along with the beer. Once bubbling nicely, turn the heat down low and cook slowly with a lid on for around 45 minutes until cooked through. Keep an eye on it. You don't want the pan to dry out, so add a little water if the beer disappears.
- Once the chicken is done, remove it to a plate. Any liquid left in the pot can be added to a jug and topped up with hot stock to make two mugs worth of liquid.
- Now you can sort out the rice. Turn the heat up a little and add the onion and carrot. Sauté for five-ten minutes until softened. You will need to give the pot a good scraping with a wooden spoon to get up all the lovely caramelised chicken bits. They're the best!
- Now add the allspice, thyme, kidney beans, and rice. Stir everything together to combine, then add your two mugs worth of stock (or lovely juices and stock combo) along with the creamed coconut.
- Stir well, bring to the boil. Place your chicken pieces on top, pop on the lid, turn the heat down low, and let it cook gently for twelve minutes.
- Once the time's up, turn off the heat but leave well alone. The rice needs a little longer to plump up. So

have a game of Dobble, or make a salad, and come back in ten minutes (fifteen won't hurt) to dish up.

Enjoy!

From the Author

Wow! I think Max and Anxious might need a rest after the festival of fear. It's making me nervous about the music festivals we have lined up for this summer. Who am I kidding? No way am I missing out on the chance to chill in a field, watch some amazing bands, and see if I can beat my record for holding my breath and not touching anything as I make a morning dash to the drop toilets before anyone else is up! The things we do to have a break.

What's next for Max and Anxious? Time to find out...

Continue Max's Campervan Case Files in Stewed to the Bone! This time, Max is salivating over food, picking up a few choice ingredients for some stunning one-pot wonders, and getting embroiled in a very grisly murder mystery at a campsite like no other. You didn't really think the next book would just be the guys chilling and playing Uno did you? Speaking of card games. Has anyone played Exploding Kittens? No? It's a lot of fun, and perfect in the campervan on rainy days or for festivals. Don't worry, no actual cats were harmed in the making of this game. Apparently...

Be sure to stay updated about new releases and fan sales. You'll hear about them first. No spam, just book updates at www.authortylerrhodes.com.

You can also follow me on Amazon www.amazon.com/stores/author/B0BN6T2VQ5.

Connect with me on Facebook www.facebook.com/authortylerrhodes/

Printed in Great Britain
by Amazon